SAVING PLANET SOQUIL

M F KATORI

Chapter 1

'I love you mum'

They were the last words Maggie Tuckett remembered saying to her mum as she rushed out of the door. She was late for school again! Maggie was supposed to be meeting her friend Lucy on the corner of Chalfont Road, they were going to walk the rest of the way to school together.

'Hi Maggie' she heard Tom say as she passed his gate, and then POP THUD BANG the world went black. Maggie heard a gasp and a hand reached out for hers.

'What's happening?' she heard herself say in a nervous voice.

'I don't know' said an equally nervous Tom gripping her hand so tightly she thought it might drop off. They were 11 years old and in their last year at Thornton first school.

They could hear a whistling sound like air rushing so fast around them. It seemed to go on forever, but it wasn't cold, and they couldn't feel any breeze. In fact, Maggie felt nothing except Tom's hand, apart from not knowing what was happening Maggie wasn't scared anymore. She was surprisingly calm. Somehow Maggie knew she was safe, and Tom's hand was no longer squeezing hers. Neither of them spoke - there was nothing to say.

They landed on a planet called WAYA area 252. It was 2 years later, neither of them knew how they got there they just seemed to arrive. They woke up one day and there they were. It was early evening and it was already dark the sky was so clear it was teaming with stars and the planet had two moons. You could see the rings around them. The sky was a mix of red and purples and the air smelt of lemons and olives, it was the nicest smell Maggie had ever smelt. She somehow knew she was home. Home! That's when Maggie realised, she would probably never see her mother nor her friend Lucy again. Maggie remembered feeling sad about that, terribly sad, and she could sense that Tom was feeling the same way. Maggie was just about to reassure him that everything was going to be OK, when a wispy figure floated towards them.

'Hi, I'm Nimb' she said, 'you are a little later than we expected, but no matter, follow me, I'll take you to see professor Detronomy. She will explain everything, then we can get you settled in'.

Professor Detronomy was just as wispy as Nimb. They were almost ghostlike, but you could see their faces, they had silky flowing gowns covering their bodies, the colours were blues, yellows and purples. They really were magnificent to look at.

'Come take a seat' said the Professor, 'I expect you are both wondering why you are here? You are what we call protectors, every planet has them even though not many people know we exist'. Both Maggie and Tom looked at each other in confusion.

'Protectors?' they both said.

'Yes' said the Professor – 'You two are both "Auras". I'm expecting you are seeing us as wispy, brightly coloured figures? Not everybody sees us the same way but you will learn all about that in your lessons. Every planet needs protecting from the pollution and damage that the inhabitants reek on their planets, there are around two hundred protectors on each planet, give or take a few depending on the planets' size. They have different gifts or abilities if you like, you two as I said are AURAS, you see the colours and vibrations that these harmful substances create, most inhabitants cannot see the colour of gasses and pollution and so therefore do not know it is there. At this school you have people that can sense, see, hear, smell or feel the danger before it happens and so therefore can stop disasters ever occurring'.

'We will teach you how to deal with these dangers, how to tap into your abilities, if you will let us. The universe needs beings like yourselves to protect it. If you don't feel you are ready or even want to then we can send you back. You will arrive as if you never left and will not remember this conversation or anything that has happened since you left Earth. If you choose to stay then your existence will be sort of erased from the minds of your family and friends and everyone that ever knew you. They will have a feeling that they once knew someone like you and think fondly for a moment at the thought of it, but they won't be sad at the loss because they won't be able to bring that memory to the surface. It won't be tangible it will just be fleetingly brief and as quickly as it came it will be gone. If however, you do meet again, then the memories will come back. We do it like this on all parties, yourselves included. That way it will be easier to concentrate on the matters in hand, the greater good as it were. It is a lot to take in I know, but unfortunately you do have to decide now as the longer you stay the less likely we are able to get you back at the exact moment you left'.

Maggie decided to stay. Tom on the other hand had a very close family - mother, father many siblings, uncles, aunts, cousins. He just couldn't bear the thought of them forgetting him in that way or, he them for that matter. Maggie on the other hand had her mum and Lucy and that was it. She felt that her life had been leading up to this, that there was a purpose for her to fulfil, which is probably why Maggie never made strong connections on Earth. Being here on Waya just felt right. Maggie said goodbye to Tom and told him to look out for her mum and Lucy, even though she knew he wouldn't remember any of this. Maggie somehow hoped a part of him would subconsciously know and through him there would be an unknown bond connecting them.

The professor told Maggie more about the school and gave her her timetable...

Monday	Tuesday	Wednesday
9am – 10:45 Aura	9am – 10:45 Aura	9am – 10:45 Aura
15 min Break	15 min Break	15 min Break
11am – 12pm Aura	11am – 12pm Aura	11am – 12pm Aura
Lunch	Lunch	Lunch
1pm – 2pm Audient	1pm – 2pm Vision	1pm – 2pm Feeling
2pm – 3pm Scent	2pm – 3pm Flava	2pm – 3pm Herbal
3pm – 5pm Homework	3pm – 5pm Homework	3pm – 5pm Home work
5pm – 6pm Dinner	5pm – 6pm Dinner	5pm – 6pm Dinner
Free Time	Free Time	Free Time
9:30pm Lights out	9:30pm Lights out	9:30pm Lights out
Thursday	**Friday**	**Saturday**
9am – 10:45 Aura	9am – 10:45 Aura	Free Time
15 min Break	15 min Break	10:30pm Lights out
11am – 12pm Aura	11am – 12pm Aura	
Lunch	Lunch	
1pm – 2pm Meditation	1pm – 2pm Herbal	**Sunday**
2pm – 3pm Mind Combat	2pm – 3pm Meditation	
3pm – 5pm Homework	3pm – 5pm Homework	10:00am – 11:45 Chapel
5pm – 6pm Dinner	5pm – 6pm Dinner	12:00 – 1:30pm Banquet Lunch
Free Time	Free Time	Free Time
9:30pm Lights out	10:00pm Lights out	9:30pm Lights out

Then Nimb took Maggie to the dining hall, Maggie was suddenly very hungry. Nimb sat her with the other Auras and asked the prefect Oswald to make sure she was introduced to the others and accompanied to her dorm with the other 1st years after dinner. Maggie discovered that not everybody looked like her, or like each other for that matter, but then again why would they? They were all from different planets.

The girl sat next to Maggie was soon to become Maggie's best friend for life, her name was Adalouisala.

'I know it's a bit of a mouthful' she said 'just call me Addy for short'. She had wild afro hair, blue skin with faint brownish black spots, she was fascinating to look at. She also had extremely long fingers and tongue, which shot out and grabbed a cake mid-sentence.

'Sorry' she said sheepishly 'I just simply love these space cakes, they make you feel all calm and sleepy they are fab just before bed, you have to try one'.

That is when Maggie discovered that there was food from every continent on Earth and she presumed from all the other planets also. The spread really was something and Addy was right, the space cakes really did make Maggie feel calm and relaxed. Maggie was feeling ready for her bed as the feast was coming to an end. Oswald took the newbies to their dorm. Addy and Maggie chose a room together that was already occupied by two other girls. Alice who was also from Earth and Angeleek who was from Soquil. She was tall, lean and very exotic looking. That night Maggie slept like a baby dreaming of food, wispy figures and exotic beings from all universes. she was home. She was where she was always meant to be. Maggie felt content for the first time ever and ready to embark on the rest of her life here on WAYA.

****

Chapter 2

'Seeoh, welcome' said Professor Detronomy. Maggie and the other 1st years had a newbies assembly welcoming them and introducing them to their head of house. They learned that they would have lessons in EVERY craft. Half the day would be with their natural gift, the other half split between the other senses. Professor Detronomy said that they would have noticed this on their timetable.

Maggie looked at Addy and shrugged her shoulders to let Addy know she hadn't even looked. Addy shook her head and then placed her head into her hands in mock disgust. They also needed to learn about Herbalism, natural medicine, good clean living with no additives. This would help keep their senses heightened and would come in handy if they got injured whilst out on missions. Addy looked at Maggie in mock terror again, she really did make Maggie laugh. Apparently, it would take a full term to detox their bodies from all the nasties they had put into them up to now so they should expect a slow start to their senses kicking in. It was explained that no matter how long it took each of them to get there, their bodies were put on hold, so no food or drink had gone in or come out so to speak, hence why it would still take time to purify their bodies. Addy and Maggie looked at each other and wrinkled their noses and did silent 'ewww' faces. Because Maggie was vegetarian, she could expect this to happen sooner than the meat-eaters amongst them.

The Professor explained that developing your senses was something that everyone can do – it is simply a matter of learning to recognise your prominent gift at work and fine tuning it to revitalise the connection between you and the other energies around you, hence why everyone had to learn about the other crafts as well.

'To be the best you can be at your gift you need to be able to use all the senses together' she said. 'The Auras in that respect had it easy as they rely on all their senses anyway'

'Result!' said Addy.

'My thoughts exactly' remarked Maggie.

They were dismissed and their head of houses took them to their first lesson. Maggie and Addy's Aura teacher was called Madam Perdido. She, like all the teachers they had met so far was wispy and floated with ease as she led them to what would be their main classroom for the coming years.

As they walked along there was a hum of quiet chatter amongst the students. Maggie leant over to Addy and asked what 'Seeoh' meant?

As if Madam Perdido heard their conversation from all the way at the front of the line she replied, 'Some of you are probably unfamiliar with the term "Seeoh". It is a polite greeting here on WAYA. You should all get used to greeting each other in this manner as it has warmth and conviction behind it – WAYA is a peaceful planet and Seeoh makes us feel at one with each other'.

Addy turned to Maggie and said, 'I think we have just had our first lesson'! Madam Perdido turned and winked at them both. Maggie knew in that instance that nothing they did was going to get passed their teachers.

In their classroom the tables were set in groups of four, Maggie and Addy sat down together at a table, second row back from the front and in the centre. They saw Angeleek and Alice and summoned them over. When everyone was settled, Madam Perdido came around with work and note books. The stationary was already on their tables, along with bags - one for each of them with the word '**AURAS'** written in bold on the front. The bag was emerald green and the word AURAS was written in purple and had a shimmering white/lilac haze around it. They found out later that the other houses had similar bags but in different colours and with their own houses written on the front.

The school didn't have uniforms as such, but their accessories had their house logos on them, bags, aprons, gowns and jumpers and t-shirts for if they left the school campus. They also had to wear their gowns at special events, functions and to the chapel on a Sunday.

'Purple and green are my favourite colours' said Maggie to the girls.

'Mine too' they all replied – in fact the entire class said the same thing, everybody smiled at their similarities.

'Before we start our lesson, we will have a cup of tea, you may chat quietly amongst yourselves'

A tea pot and cups were brought to each table by Nimb.

'It is a stimulating tonic' announced Nimb 'to aid you in your studies'. The tea was an infusion of:

- Aven Sativa (wild oats)
- Hypericum Perforatum (St John's-wort)
- Turnera Diffusa (Damiana)
- Salvia Officinalis (Sage)
- Artemisia Valgaris (Mugwort)

They all sipped their tea – and felt their brains engage. The colours around the class room seemed to shift from natural vision to H.D. The teapots and cups were removed, and the lesson began.

'Before you came here you probably were aware you felt certain situations more strongly than others - those with gifts do. We feel deep compassion for others, we can sense their energy. You are too young at the moment to understand the heart, but we also love more deeply. We are in tune with each other's' flow and energies. We have been using our energy since time began, craft was passed down to craft, but over the years our need to use our sixth sense has been laid to rest by most people. Languages developed, and as we became more civilized, we lost the ability to use it - well most did, but it is always there. You know a phone will ring before it does and who it will be before you answer it. That is your sixth sense working away in the background without you even realising its even there. You naturally warm to people you like and know you can trust – drawn together like opposite ends of a magnet. Turn that magnet around and that is the feeling you get when you don't like or trust someone, again your sixth sense at work, but people have stopped relying on these senses so they only realize someone is untrustworthy or that they actually are not their cup of tea when it is too late and a connection has been made. If they had listened to their senses, then they would have saved themselves an awful lot of heartache - like our sixth sense, we don't need certain body parts any more either – your appendix for example'.

Maggie looked at Addy she was pulling a pained face and raising her eyebrows and was holding her stomach where her appendix would be. Maggie had to put her hand over her mouth to stifle a laugh.

'Our bodies have evolved like our minds, yet it is still there in your body, you would think that if you didn't have a use for it anymore then we simply would be born without it! So why are we born with it? Who knows? Maybe one day we will have use for it again, just like maybe one day, with the way the inhabitants treat their planets, they will have a use for their sixth sense again. When their planet is on the brink of extinction maybe. Who knows? What we do know is that there are a handful of people from each planet that have heightened senses – like you lot - and we intend to teach you how to use them to the best of your abilities'

'There have been disasters before. The Ice Age for example, and mother nature carried on giving. If there were another disaster, at least we know she will be there supplying us with what we need to survive. We will use herbs for cooking and medicines again. We will show you also how to use these herbs, for nutritional and medicinal use. That way if a planet does fall at the inhabitant's hands you will be able to show them the way back. Usually we can step in and help fix a problem before it becomes a disaster, unbeknown to the inhabitants, working behind the scenes, so you don't even get an acknowledgement or a thank you - but that is the way we like it. After all we don't want another witch hunt, another Salem!'

'Let's do a group activity. I want you to choose a person from another table, then working in groups of four, two

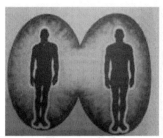

'A Mingle'

'A Combine'

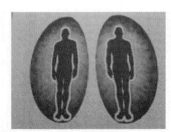

'A Repel'

people from your table and two from another I would like you to stand in pairs - one person from your table and one from another to start. I want you to see if you can read each other's Auras. You will see three different positions. If your Aura likes but does not know the person standing next to you, then you should get what we call "A̲ mingle". If you are not drawn to each other, you will see "A̲ repel". And if you then stand with your friend from your table you should see "A̲ combine". I would like you to write down each pairings Aura position. Don't worry about colour just yet, just concentrate on the positions'

The class worked like this for the rest of the lesson. It was really interesting watching people's Auras shift from 'A̲ mingle' to 'A̲ combine' as they became friends over the exercise. By the end of the lesson only two people remained 'A̲ repel' - a girl from AWI called Janwa and a boy from Yona whose name was impossible to pronounce so everyone just called him Dave!

Madam Perdido explained that sometimes at this age those of the opposite sex had 'A̲ repel because their bodies actually liked each other, and their minds couldn't work these feelings out. Their Aura's repelled each other until their minds caught up with their bodies. Then they would become soul mates for life and, given this was a peaceful planet this was probably what was happening here. Janwa and Dave did not like this idea and their Auras jumped even further apart. The whole class laughed causing even more embarrassment for the pair. Madam Perdido chuckled and told everyone to take a fifteen-minute break. Maggie noticed in that break that Janwa and Dave were checking each other out, she smiled to herself but did not draw attention to it.

After their break they played with each other's energy some more, seeing how far apart they could get from a partner and still feel their Aura. By the end of the lesson Maggie could identify three quarters of the class with her eyes closed. Madam Perdido said this had never been done in one of her classes with a first year before and asked her to stay behind after the lesson had ended.

Addy, Angeleek and Alice were waiting outside the class for her when she came out.

'What did she say?' asked Addy.

'Apparently there is a progressive mind combat club on a Sunday afternoon, she wants me to join it. I told her I'll think about it. She told me she would speak to Oswald and suggested I get a book from the library. We have mind combat on a Thursday and she said she is going to tell Dan about me'. Said Maggie

'Dan? Who's Dan' asked Addy.

'He's our mind combat coach apparently',.

'You have to do it' said Alice, 'Let's go to the library now before lunch'.

****

Chapter 3

The next few days passed quickly. Maggie noticed she was quite good at, and liked most of her lessons, which shocked her really because on Earth she found lessons boring and a waste of time. It dawned on her that she must have subconsciously known there was more important things at play.

In her Aroma class she was at the same level as most of the year twos. Professor Aviral wondered if she should be in her house instead of the Auras, but Maggie knew Auras was where she was meant to be. In fact, Maggie was somewhere near the top in all of her classes except Flava, which considering part of tasting food is through smell was a little odd.

'If you don't like the smell of something you are about to eat you are less likely to try it' explained Professor Cook (aptly named) Maggie could smell, people, food, danger and excitement so vividly, yet trying to taste it with her senses just wasn't happening.

'Your sense of taste is very bland' said Professor Cook. 'No wonder you are so skinny'.

'Wow' said Addy quietly 'that was uncalled for, but it is actually quite nice to be better than you at something' she said shouting 'VANILLA' and winning yet another treat as they played guess the flavour.

At dinner that evening Maggie couldn't believe that Addy was still piling her plate full after everything she had already eaten. Addy looked at Maggie's plate and said 'Professor Cook has a point' then jibed her playfully in the belly.

Maggie read quite a lot about mind combat over the next few days and tried some of the activities. She actually really did enjoy it and by Thursday afternoon had already made her mind up before the lesson that she would give progressive mind combat a go. Maggie caught Oswald in the corridor before her lesson and told him she would come along on Sunday.

'Cool. We shall be having try outs on Sunday so it will be interesting to see if you are as good as Perdido says - who knows maybe you will make the team'.

'No pressure' Maggie thought as she slipped into what was going to become her favourite class of all time ever.

Maggie soon learnt the rules of the game:

- The game was played in total darkness.

- You only had your senses to guide you.
- There were seven players on each team.
- The idea was to get to the opposite side in the fastest time.
- The other team members were supposed to block you.

They weren't the only obstructions though – there were waterfalls, tight ropes, sinking sand, wild dogs and boulders dropping, and that was only the school team, The professionals had it far worse!!

The class didn't start the game with a match - they navigated their way around the obstacles. Maggie was the fastest in the class to get from one side to the other by far. Dan, who was not actually a teacher but used to play for Waya Warriors had agreed to coach Mind Combat, was also from Earth. He pulled the next three fastest in the class and told them they now had to try and stop Maggie. Maggie thought It was so much fun. It was both frightening and exhilarating at the same time and her heart was pounding in her ears. By the end of the class Maggie was getting around seven other class members and Dan said she would make the team without a doubt. When they were not playing, they got to watch the others through infra-red goggles. Addy was so bad it was comical, Maggie had the feeling that Addy knew how bad she was and was playing on it. 'Safe to say she will not be making the team' Angeleek whispered and we both chuckled. Angeleek was very agile and Dan suggested that she too should try the progressive club on Sunday. Alice wasn't too bad but not quite good enough for progressive. Maybe she would make the year one house team, with a bit more practise - if not then she should definitely make the reserves. Thought Maggie.

That evening at dinner Maggie's plate was full for the first time ever. It was piled as high as Addy's.

'Someone has worked up an appetite' Addy said through a mouthful of food.

'You are such a lady' Angeleek said shaking her head in mock disgust and the four of them laughed. Maggie really loved it on WAYA. Her life felt complete and like it was leading somewhere. That night while the others slept, all she could think of was mind combat and how she couldn't wait until Sunday.

Sunday soon arrived. The year ones had their first Sunday service in the chapel. It was breath-taking. There was a gigantic tree in the middle of the chapel with colours so stunning. Maggie had never seen anything like it. She could see threads of silk in different colours stretching out around the room encompassing some of the people, and an almost inaudible whisper coming from them. These were souls who had passed on. The tree was in fact the tree of life. The souls were using the trees' energy to reconnect with their loved ones. Suddenly one of the whispers became clear as crystal and Maggie was both shocked and pleased to hear her grandfather's voice in her head. she didn't have to speak back to him with her voice she was having a telepathic conversation with him. When it was time to go everybody held hands and thanked the tree and their loved ones for connecting with them. Maggie's heart was so full of joy she left the chapel feeling overwhelmed and uplifted all at the same time.

Next they all went on to the dining hall to share in a Sunday banquet. The day so far was so full of love and joy that Maggie almost forgot about the progressive combat training until Angeleek tapped her on the shoulder and asked if she was ready.

'Oh no, I wish I'd not eaten so much' Maggie groaned.

On the way to the hall Angeleek asked about Maggie's message and Maggie asked if she had spoken to anyone. Angeleek said that she had never lost anyone close to her, and that when she did get a message it would be a mix of emotions as she would then know that someone had passed over.

'At least we have the tree of souls though' she said. 'That will make it more comforting.'

As they reached the progressive combat training hall, they recognised lots of other Auras. As Auras are gifted in all crafts, they can sense energy quicker than most – unlike an Aroma for example who is predominantly only gifted with the sense of smell - even though with training they can learn the other crafts. They will never be as natural as an Aura.

Angeleek and Maggie were the only two from year 1. Oswald put everyone through their paces and at the end of the warm-up the other craft leaders including Oswald chose their teams for the year. Ten players on each team - seven players and three reserves. Maggie and Angeleek made the team, they hugged each other and jumped up and down in excitement.

'Next week we will have a match against each other and the star player from each team will definitely represent the school in outer school competitions' Oswald announced. 'The rest of the team will be picked on merit'.

'I bet you make the team' Angeleek said.

'I doubt it. Surely the team leaders will' Maggie replied.

'They don't get to play in their final year - they have too many exams, so they coach the rest of the team instead' said Angeleek.

Maggie's mind went into excitement overload. 'How come you know so much?' she asked.

'My brother Gabriel is here. He left Soquil two years ago. I'd almost forgotten about him until I bumped into him in the hallway earlier today' said Angeleek.

'Wow!' exclaimed Maggie and she wondered if she had any siblings here. 'I bet that was a shock'.

'It was lovely' said Angeleek. 'We didn't particularly get on when we lived together, but the reconnection was amazing. It feels nice to have someone here'.

When they got back to the dorm Maggie told Addy about Angeleek and Addy said 'I have a feeling I have a sibling here too. There is a strong sense of belonging and it grows every time I think he or she is near. I read in "A HISTORY OF WAYA" that apparently there are lots of brothers and sisters that reconnect here - after all the gift runs in families. Mostly they just bump into each other in the halls or where ever and BAM - it's like they were never apart'.

'I don't get that feeling at all' said Maggie and she was pensive for a while.

'At least you got to speak to someone from the tree of souls' Addy said as if she could feel Maggie's momentary sadness. And just like that Maggie felt better.

Later that evening at supper there was an announcement that there was going to be an ALL-STAR MIND COMBAT match held here in WAYA in a fortnights time, and anyone who got on the team was allowed to leave campus under Dans' supervision to go and watch.

'I know what I shall be doing every spare moment' Maggie said to Angeleek.

'Me too' she replied, and the pair high fived.

Addy and Alice both said, 'Looks like we won't be hanging with you guys for a while'. We all laughed and went off to our dorms. It was a very enjoyable first week, Maggie looked at her friends and her heart soared. Life on WAYA was good – very good.

****

Chapter 4

"AURIC EGG"

This was written on the board in front of us when we arrived at our Aura class Monday morning.

'Inside this egg' the Professor began 'are lines of force and energy which radiate in all directions. They reflect a person's thought process, their feelings, health and potentials. Your Aura is made up of energy fields that flow at right angles, the first flow up and down at vertical directions, the second horizontal and around the body and finally other energies emanate from the spine and head to outer extremities. All these energy lines criss-cross and create a mesh of interwoven magnetic energy. Most people at some point in their lives have seen what is known as the ready brek glow'

"Auric Egg"

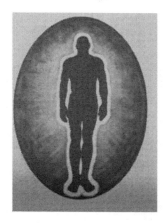

'However, the Aura also contains colour. This is believed to be what Sir Isaac Newton saw and was the first to demonstrate to the lay person in 1666 when he observed the sunlight through a glass prism creating a rainbow effect. Like all people ahead of their time Newton was ridiculed for this, but this didn't stop him carrying on with his studies. He then went on to pass light through two prisms. Light from the first prism divided up into a rainbow. This rainbow turned back clear after passing through the second prism. Thus, showing that the colour was already in the prism - the sunlight had just picked up what was already there. Also, we think of black and white as colours, but they are in fact just opposite polarities of light and dark'

'So let's do an exercise. Rub your hands together like this and start playing with your energy ball. Bring your hands slowly together then apart until you can feel the resistance and pull of your energy and then when you are ready, with a partner, point your index finger at each other – tips touching. Slowly bring them apart concentrating on the silver white line. Don't let your concentration lapse'

'When you can all see this line with ease and still see it when standing at least two feet away from each other, come and stand around this round table. This is going to take quite a lot of concentration from you guys.'

When we were all there, Madam Perdido had us place our hands on the table with our fingers splayed apart. The table had a black shiny surface. The lights were dimmed, blinds were pulled shut and the energy flowed from all our fingertips to the person opposite, criss-crossing in the middle. It was breath taking - simply stunning.

`

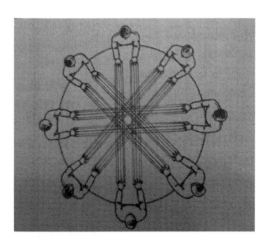

After this Nimb brought us a revitalising infusion of tea.

- Liquorice root

- Lemon grass
- Spearmint
- Apple bits

Nimbs teas always made you feel exactly how they were supposed to; the woman was a genius!

When we had finished our tea, we went around the classroom practising todays lessons with each other. Touching fingertips and playing with energy balls. The classroom was an array of colour and silver threads. We made notes on this and then as there were a few minutes left before the end of class Madam Perdido had us throwing our energy balls to each other. The classroom was like a firework display but without the noise. I was a little disappointed when the bell went.

After lunch we had our third Audient class, and as promised by Professor Meridet at Fridays class, the whole lesson was done in silence. You had to concentrate so hard to focus, and just listen to the Professor or whoever was answering a question. It really was draining.

After the lesson I said to the girls 'Remind me to ask Nimb how to make the revitalising tea'. Alice smiled and when we got back to the dorm she disappeared for a while and when she came back, she had a tray with four cups and a tea pot on it. We all stared at her.

'What' she said. 'While you guys are off at mind combat or practising for mind combat and Addy is in the library, what else am I supposed to do with my time? I asked Nimb for some hints. I like her teas' she said sheepishly.

'We are not complaining' we all said, 'and your tea is just as good as Nimbs' I added. This made Alice beam from ear to ear bless her. She really was a sensitive little soul, and her energy was so pure, calming and relaxing. She was a nice person to be around, and I felt in that instance a need to hug her, so I did and then Addy and Angeleek joined in. We rolled around on the floor laughing and getting odd looks from the other Auras in our dorm - this just made us laugh all the more.

We went down to the dining hall for dinner and then myself and Angeleek went off to practice some mind combat. We were both so desperate to go and see a real match. We were just about to pack up and go back to our dorm when we heard Professor Dan talking with Nimb in hushed voices. We didn't mean to stand and eavesdrop, but it sounded urgent and we didn't want to interrupt, so we sat in silence. Nimb was telling Dan that the mind combat trip might need to be cancelled. Her husband was on the committee and it appeared Soquil was in a worse state than first expected. Dan would probably have to go out on the mission and help repair the damage, and that would mean he couldn't accompany the students to the match.

'What a shame' said Dan 'They have all been practising so hard. I've seen Maggie and Angeleek up here three times since yesterday. They will both be disappointed'.

'I don't know what's worse' said Nimb. 'The students who know what to expect or those that have never seen a game'!

The pair wandered off deep in conversation unaware they had been overheard. When they were out of earshot, I turned to Angeleek to moan about the situation. She was just sitting there looking shocked...and then it dawned on me. She was from Soquil.

'I'm sure it will all be fine' I said trying to reassure her. I put my hand on hers until she was ready to come back to the dorm. Something told me this was a bad situation. A serious situation.

When we got back to the dorm Angeleek went straight to her room. I expected she wanted some alone time, so I took Addy and Alice to one side and filled them in.

'Oh no how terrible' said Addy. 'That's why Nimb rushed off earlier. Professor Detronomy came to her room and told her that her husband needed to talk to her urgently. He is from Soquil also'.

'How is it Addy is the one always in the library or with her nose in a book, yet you are the one that always seems to know everything?' I asked jokingly.

'I suppose it's a case of not what you know but who you know' said Alice.

'How does that work anyway?' I said.

'How does what work?' said Alice looking at me quizzically.

'You know, Nimb is from WAYA and her husband is from Soquil'

'Well I guess it's a case of boy meets girl, girl meets boy and they fall in love' said Alice shocked at my lack of intelligence in the matters of love.

'I don't mean that, I mean do they have children? Where do they live?'

'For someone so gifted you really have not got a clue have you' said Addy.

'What do you mean by that' I asked. Addy got a book out and showed me each planets inhabitants and what they looked like.

'I know that' I said. 'I've seen the different people here at the school'.

Then she showed me all the different people that lived here on WAYA. 'There are about three hundred different districts on WAYA. Nearly everyone that lives here is with someone from another planet, and so therefore their children are of mixed species – Like this' she said showing me another book.

'Oh, I see' I said. I had seen plenty of these people also at the school and just presumed they were from different planets. 'I wondered why I had never seen anyone like that on Earth' I said pointing to a child whose mother was from Earth but whose father was from Yanasai.

'Really!' Addy gasped 'You are something else. You do know that if you meet someone from another planet you won't be able to return to Earth don't you?' I hadn't even thought about it, I hadn't even thought about what would happen when I finished school let alone meeting someone. I was living in the here and now. We have people from seven different planets here yet there could be so many more planets, I just simply took it for what it was and didn't even second guess it. Maybe I should start paying a bit more attention!

'So some people must know they are going to come here then. Has Nimb got children?' I asked.

'Yes' said Alice. 'She has three - one boy who works for the council with his dad, another boy - you might know him - he is head of the Flava combat team. His name is Brad, after Brad Pitt. Nimb fancies Brad Pitt' she chuckled 'and a daughter who should be starting here next year but as yet she isn't showing any real gifts'.

'Wow that must be hard for her if the rest of the family are so gifted'

'I know' said Alice 'but Nimb said if she hasn't got it then she hasn't got it. There is more to life then being a protector! Nimb really didn't seem too fussed'.

I thought about the conversation for a while, and how I had been so wrapped up in my studies that I hadn't been very observant, when Angeleek came back down stairs.

'Are you ok?' said Addy.

'I'm not sure' said Angeleek. 'I think I need to know what is going on. I'm going to see Nimb'.

'Wait we will come too. Anything we can do to help, we want to be there for you. We are all in this together - one for all and all for one' Alice said. I smiled at the reference, Addy and Angeleek just looked at each other not even bothering to be puzzled by our Earthling sayings any more. And we all went off to Nimbs.

****

Chapter 5

'It is true' said Nimb, 'There are problems on Soquil at the moment, but I don't know how you girls have found out about this'. Myself and Angeleek glanced at each other. 'There really is nothing for you to worry about – it would be also very much appreciated if you didn't discuss this in public. We don't want the rest of the school getting their knickers in a twist like you lot'.

'Of course we will keep it to ourselves, but Angeleek's family are from Soquil' I said.

'I think I can see that Maggie, but like I said it isn't that serious. Things like this happen all the time, and a team goes in and sorts it out. Most of the time the inhabitants are even unaware. Now off you go and stop your worrying'.

'So if it is nothing to worry about then why might the mind combat trip be cancelled' I protested.

'Because Professor Dan is a member of the mission team. If and I mean IF we are needed to deploy, then there will be nobody to take you. Now off you go, it really does no good to worry. Why don't you make them a nice pot of tea for anxiety' Nimb said to Alice and with a knowing smile suggested half a teaspoon more of the main ingredient as she ushered us all out of the room.

When we got back to the dorm Alice went off to make some tea.

'I'm sorry to say it' I said, mainly to Angeleek, 'but I have a bad feeling about this'

'I'm with you on that' said Angeleek.

'I will loiter in the Hall of Minds tomorrow' said Addy.

'The hall of what?' I said.

'Minds' said Addy shaking her head as she so often did at me. 'You get snippets of all sorts of information from there. Souls of past and present have deep mind conversations there. If there is any more information that is where I will find it'. At that moment Alice came back with a pot of tea, and whatever the main ingredient was it worked a treat, knocked us all for six. We slept soundly until morning. We almost never made it to breakfast.

Nimb caught up with us in our Aura class and told us that Professor Detronomy wanted to see us and that we should head up there before lunch.

'Great' said Alice, 'Now we are in trouble'

But we were soon to find out that we were far from it. Professor Detronomy told us she wanted us to attend the missions meeting in the dining hall. It was in the middle of our Flava's class so she would get us a pass. What a result I thought.

Detronomy turned to me looked me straight in the eye and said 'Don't think this gets you out of it though. Addy can pick up the class synopsis and fill you in with what you will have missed later'. I felt my heart sink as Addy's soared. She was so pleased that the Professor thought her capable of teaching us what we missed. She was proud of the task the Head had bestowed on her. I suddenly felt really happy because *she* was so happy and I felt Angeleek lift also. She was about to find out just how much or little her planet was in danger.

We went and grabbed a bite to eat, all of us deep in thought about the meeting. Three of us not having a clue what to expect, Addy on the other hand knowing a surprising amount. It dawned on me that I really should read more and maybe take the time to people-watch, but my mind was always full of the next task. I found it really hard in Meditation to focus.

'You will burn out' declared Willow at one of our meditation classes 'if you don't learn to let go'. I decided there and then to practice at least ten minutes a day.

The Audient class went so slowly. As soon as Professor Meridet thought 'You can go now', I was out of the chair and on my way to the dining hall.

'Hey hold up!' shouted the others 'I'm sure they won't start without us'.

When we got to the hall a lot of people were already seated while I headed towards Nimb and Dan. If I was going to be here I wanted to hear what they had to say. I noticed Angeleek wander off. I looked over my shoulder and saw her brother Gabriel was here too. I turned to speak to Addy and noticed her gazing off over the opposite side of the hall. I followed her eyeline and saw a girl waving at her.

'Who is that?' I said.

Addy gasped and waved back and with a tear in her eye she managed to choke out 'Wow it's my sister Evannah. How could I ever have forgotten her - look how beautiful she is'.

I looked over the hall and sure enough her sister was stunning, so vibrant. She had the same wild hair as Addy, but she was much leaner.

'I'm so sorry to leave you girls but I have to go and say hello'.

'No, no you go' we both replied 'You must. You will have so much to catch up on'.

We watched as she walked away from us, her sister was walking towards her and their Auras grew brighter and reached out to each other way before the girls made their physical embrace, it was a lovely sight to see.

'Do you think you have somebody here?' I said to Alice.

'No I don't' she said 'What about you?'

'No. I don't think so either'.

Before we had time to dwell on this the dining hall door swung open and in walked Professor Detronomy, Nimbs husband Mikka and the head of the council Lord Raybottom.

Lord Raybottom, was a tiny man, but his presence and aura were huge. They almost filled the room. What he lacked in height he made up for in importance. He welcomed the members new and old and then the meeting began. Nimb was taking notes.

'The problem on Soquil has reached a level 2' he announced. 'I think we should set a team up and go take a look. There is no real urgency just yet so I'm thinking Monday after next. What say ye?'

Yes, I said to myself and looked around the room for Angeleek. She already had eyes on me, and nodded knowingly. I was pleased about the mind combat match going ahead and I could tell she was too, but more importantly, she was a little more laid back about her planet's situation. I watched as her aura softened. I hadn't quite noticed just how firm it had become until I visibly watched it soften. She must have been much more worried then she had been letting on.

Apparently, the carbon dioxide levels were slowly starting to drop, which at first was thought to be due to the planet's population increase over the last few years. But after a few years of monitoring they have decided that there must be a small tear somewhere on the outer crust. The council were going to deploy a team to see if they could detect the tear, and cause, and then hopefully fix it unnoticed. It was announced that Dan, Mikka and Joe, who was Nimb and Mikka's son, were to head the mission and report back. The rest of us would be informed of the situation on their return. They scheduled a meeting for a months' time. Everyone started to leave, but Nimb said that Professor Detronomy wanted us to stay behind.

When the room was almost empty, the Head called us over to a table. Around the table was Detronomy, Dan, Nimb, Addy's sister Evannah and Angeleeks brother Gabriel. Professor Detronomy invited us to become members of the council.

'We don't usually have first year members, but you four are showing a great deal of individual talent that can be brought to the table' she explained. 'Talents like yours will be an asset to us. It is always good to have a host of knowledge and a range of ages on the council, that way we don't become rigid in our ways. We keep ourselves open to fresh ideas'.

'You might see things we have not thought of before as you have not been out on a mission. You will bring a fresh approach. After all we deal with people from all walks of life -

old and young, so, is it not only fair that we have all walks of life old and young on our team? If you agree it will be even more important that you participate fully in your classes. You still have so much to learn, to enable you to be fully equipped for both this and many missions to come. You can let us know at the next meeting if you wish to take on this role. You must think very carefully about this...oh and Maggie, Angeleek, I think Professor Dan has some news for you both so don't rush off'.

And with that she turned and left.

Alice went with Nimb to meet her husband and son properly, and Addy went off to chat to her sister some more. Dan smiled at us both and announced that as a treat for all the practice we had put in - and we suspected as a bribe to join the council - he had two tickets for us for the upcoming mind combat match.

'Wow thanks a lot' we both said with huge smiles, and I taught Angeleek how to high five. We were so excited.

****

Chapter 6

Angeleek and I went back to practicing mind combat every spare minute. Addy spent her spare time in the library, or the hall of minds and Alice spent a lot of her time with Nimb learning how to make teas for all ailments and occasions. She was really getting rather good. She also found out that Nimb had no real gift as such. She could use all of them marginally but was very limited. She was however a very good healer, and her herbalism was known amongst all. She could manipulate the flow of energy with her hands. When she studied at the school herself, she had been an Aura, but because she had no real talent she stayed on at the school and helped out in the Aura classes and did the occasional healing where needed.

'The females in our family had never been ones to shine' she told Alice, which was why she was not particularly fussed about her daughter Felicity - Flick for short - possessing any real talent. She would quite like her to come to the school next year, but it wasn't the be all and end all. Flick was quite often around her mothers when Alice was over and she more often than not joined in.

'If I'm not gonna be able to protect, then I might as well heal mind, body and soul like my mamma, had I not!' she exclaimed.

Alice liked Flick. She was funny, maybe a little rebellious at times, but very, very funny and never malicious.

The day of the interschool team announcements was upon us. We went to the chapel and I had a lovely chat with my grandad again and told him all about it. As it happened, he told me that he also went to this school and was also on the council, on the mission squad, and was also on the combat team. He could have gone professional, but he had a mission on Earth and met, and later married my nan, so obviously stayed on Earth and chose to be a protector of Earth only.

'You can do that?' I asked.

'Of course you can' said my grandfather. 'Where ever your life takes you, you go. You still get to live your life, protector or not'.

'I really don't know what I want to do beyond this school' , I said.

'You have plenty of time for all that' my grandfather said. 'And besides, destiny has a way of steering you on to the right path'.

And with that we said our goodbyes, thanked the tree of souls and went for our Sunday feast.

I told the girls I wanted to be part of the council and wanted to go out on missions. Angeleek said the same. Addy wanted to be a part of the council on the research team and Alice knew she wanted to be part of it but was unsure where her role would sit.

'You two have hardly eaten' Addy said to both Angeleek and me.

'I think we are both too nervous' I said.

Alice made us a tea infusion that really helped. We both went off to the progressive mind combat with a new-found confidence. We really gave it our all, and at the end of the session the team was picked. Even though Angeleek and I knew we were going to the match, we both really wanted to be on the team. We sat silently as Oswald made the announcement.

Yes, my name was the first to be called out along with six others. I felt Angeleeks energy shift to disappointment when her name wasn't called out and I went to place my hand over hers to comfort her, but just as my hand reached hers, her name was called as first reserve. We both cheered and when the final two reserves were announced we congratulated each other. Then, myself and Angeleek went off to find Addy and Alice to let them know the good news.

We found Addy first. She was just coming out of the Hall of Minds. She looked deep in thought but quickly shifted when she saw us.

'You got in then' she announced.

'How did you know?' we gasped.

'I have my sources' she said pointing behind her at the Hall of Minds. 'Its not what you know its who you know remember – speaking of which, where is Alice?'

'Probably at Nimbs, let's go find her' Angeleek said.

As we walked up to Nimbs front door we heard peals of laughter and hysterical giggling.

Nimb answered the door and said 'I am afraid Flick is bringing the very worst out in your friend. You best come in and save her'.

We all looked at each other a little confused.

'Flick is my daughter' Nimb explained, and then shouted to Flick and Alice that Alice had company.

'Come' we heard Alice say to what must have been Flick. 'Let me introduce you to my friends'.

As they rounded the corner, Flick came to an abrupt halt and stared at Addy square in the eyes, Addy was staring back in the same manner. Nimb rolled her eyes and smiled to herself shaking her head knowingly. Alice broke the intensity by introducing Flick to us. We told Alice and Nimb our news, and they congratulated us. Flick thought that was really cool, and then Nimb said it was getting late and that we should be heading back to our dorms.

When we were back and Angeleek and Alice were out of earshot, I asked Addy what that was all about?

'What?' she said, but she knew what I meant.

'I think we just imprinted on each other' she said with her head in her hands

'Imprinted?' I said

'Yes' said Addy. 'It's what two souls who are destined to be together do. It's more than soul mates, its like twin flames, "split aparts". Our souls have just interlocked. We will be whatever each other wants us to be until such a time that we are old enough to be together. Like together, together'.

'Oh' I said. 'And how do you feel about that?'

'I think I'm ok with it, at least we will not have any of the games that other couples have as we are destined to be together. We wont ever be second guessing each other. But did you see Nimb clock us?'

'Yes I did and she seemed really happy, probably for the same reasons you have just said. At least she knows her daughter will never be messed about'.

'Well that would be a relief' said Addy. 'I feel like she is my reason for existing, and I hers. Imagine how awful it would be if her family didn't approve'.

'Well I don't think you will need to worry about that'

'No true, and at the moment I think we are both going to be just good friends, so we might as well get to know each other. And Maggie - for now can you not say anything to the others?'

'Of course not. You can tell them in your own time, although I think Alice noticed something. If you need to talk about this Addy then please feel free. I'm here for you always'

'I know you are' said Addy, and we hugged.

When the others came back, Addy announced she had some information from the Hall of Minds regarding Soquil. 'I didn't know if right now was the time to say anything, with you two just receiving your combat news' she said to Angeleek and I, 'but I overheard a conversation in the Hall of Minds today. TAHLEQUAH is preparing for an influx of souls'

'TAHLEQUAH?', I asked.

'Yes' said Addy 'It's like Heaven. Paradise. Whatever you want to call it. It's where the souls go when they leave their mortal bodies'.

We all gasped.

'I didn't catch all the conversation, just bits and pieces. The other souls or people seem to know you are listening, so it is very tricky to eavesdrop without drawing attention to yourself'

'But I heard someone from the other side saying that there was a hole in the outer crust', she continued 'and the rate the rotations were spinning, the planet may well not be there in five years' time. The tear in the outer crust we already know about, but then someone else responded that there was another tear in the middle layer. Every time the two line up, a gust of wind is making the hole bigger, letting carbon monoxide leak in, and oxygen leak out. Apparently, those living closer to it are already suffering from poor health'.

'You need to tell Professor Detronomy' we all said urgently.

'I don't think this should wait until the next meeting' I said.

'It will be lights out in a bit' said Addy, 'I'll go to the library in the break tomorrow and see if I can find out what might be happening, then we can go and see the Head at lunch. It might just be rumours. This is why the council like to keep things quiet.'

Angeleek sighed and rubbed her temples 'I don't think it is a rumour. My nan spoke to me and Gabe on Sunday. All we heard was "Save your planet. Save your family", but we both heard it'.

'Oh no Angeleek. Why didn't you say anything?'

'I don't know. It just seemed a bit odd. Neither of us felt like she had actually passed over. It seemed like just a message, but now this! It could be more'.

None of us slept very well that night. I decided we should see Professor Detronomy in our fifteen-minute break. She opened the door before we even knocked and told us to come in and take a seat. I still found it unnerving when people did that - knew you were coming before you got there. It was slightly odd. Addy told the head what she had learned, and then Angeleek told her about her grandmother.

'Hmm yes' said Detronomy. 'We have heard this information too and was going to bring it up at the next meeting. It is predicted that if nothing is done, the planet could be sucked into the abyss within the next five years. It has been reported that those closest to the tear are slipping into unknown comas and this is how the messages are being relayed. Sorry to say Angeleek, but your grandmother must be one of these victims. She was a very talented Aura in her time, which is how she would have been able to come through to you'

'We need to go in and repair it before it gets worse', she continued. 'No one has died yet, and we don't know if the coma victims will regain consciousness. We have still, however, decided to leave the date of the mission where it as as we will need the help of the scientists on Soquil. We will be better received by the inhabitants when they realise they have a problem - they will be more likely to help'.

'Please try not to worry Angeleek, and if you or your brother hear anything else come and see me night or day. I'll tell your head of house and teachers that you both have a pass to leave your lessons or dorm after lights out. I will inform Lord Raybottom about this meeting and let you all know if anything changes, although I suspect not as it really is nothing we are not already aware of. Thanks for coming to see me. Awaula'.

'Awaula' I said when we all left the room.

'Goodbye', Addy informed us. It's supposed to make you feel less nervous or intimidated either after bad news or a conflict'. 'How are you feeling Angeleek?'

'I think I need to go and find Gabe and tell him what's been said. I'm not happy about my nan being in a coma, but at least we have her to converse with. I'll see you guys in class'

'Ok. Awaula' I said.

Angeleek nodded in appreciation at the sentiment.

****

Chapter 7

When Angeleek got back to class she said her brother was going to talk to Madam Perdido about having some extra Aura lessons. He wanted to go out on the mission to Soquil. He had suggested that me and Angeleek should do the same

'Do you think Detronomy would allow us?' I said. 'Don't you think we are a bit young?'

'That is why Gabe said, "Let's have some extra lessons, so we can prove ourselves". After all, we are all on the mind combat team so we must already be doing something right, and Detronomy did say she wanted old and young minds alike'.

'Yes, but I don't think she meant we could go out on this mission. I think she just wanted us to observe, see how it's done and offer our opinions.'

'Well there is only one way to find out. I am going to ask Madam Perdido after class. It will probably also help us with our mind combat as well'.

And as soon as she said that, I was in. I suspected that was her plan to convince me all along.

After class we spoke to Madam Perdido and told her that Gabe was interested also. She thought it was a fabulous idea - three of her star pupils wanting to better themselves. We didn't tell her it was because we were hoping to go out on the upcoming mission in case she changed her mind, and so she offered us an extra forty-five minutes before dinner on a Monday and Wednesday. We pushed for a Friday also but she was a little taken aback, maybe suspicious even at our determination to get so far on in the subject considering we didn't even have major exams for another two years. But she was also flattered at the idea we enjoyed her lessons so much and so agreed.

'We can still get in plenty of practice for mind combat as well' Angeleek said when we left Perdido's room. 'It's just a matter of organising our time better.'

When we got to the dining hall, Gabe was sat with Addy, Alice and Evannah. We told Gabe what we had organised and Evannah said she wanted in too. We told her to mention it to Madam Perdido and to tell her that none of us minded her joining in. Besides, most of her classes are done in groups of two and four any way so it will work better.

When we got back to the dorm that night we sat down with Addy and Alice. Gabe and Evannah joined us and we worked on a timetable on how we could best manage our time and still get our homework and mind combat in. Addy said she would type us up an evening schedule. Angeleek, Evannah, Gabe and I would have a fifteen minute break at the end of school and on a Monday, Wednesday and a Friday would fit in an Aura lesson 3:45 – 4:30. Then have another fifteen minutes break and practice mind combat from 4:45 – 5:30. That would give us half an hour to chill out before dinner - and after dinner we would do our homework. On a Tuesday, Thursday and Saturday the four of us would set aside some time to practice whatever Madam Perdido had shown us the day before.

Addy was going to do some research in the hall of minds and the library with Nimbs' son Brad. Apparently, they had already been working together and seemed to bounce off each other well. Alice said she would spend the extra time with Nimb. She had decided that she wanted to be a healer and as we wouldn't be taking healing classes until the third year, she would ask Nimb to give her some lessons. She also said she would suggest that Flick should do the same. It might help her get into the school if she had something to offer. I felt Addy's Aura pulse at the mention of Flick's name - it was really very sweet.

Addy suggested that Alice should go and ask Flick if she wanted to join in and ask Nimb for her support, and then come back and let her know. Then she would get the timetable written up so everyone knew what they were doing. Alice was back in no time with the thumbs up, and so our little mission squad was formed. The eight of us would soon become firm friends, comrades, friends for life a real tight nit little group. We would get to know each other inside out and know that on a mission we would have each other's backs, working so close together we wouldn't even need to verbally communicate. We would just seamlessly know what each other was thinking and doing. Like the eight of us would be one mighty force to be reckoned with.

The next morning at breakfast Addy handed us our time-tables.

Angeleek, Evannah, Gabe, Maggie

After school Time Table:

Monday, Wednesday & Friday
3:45 – 4:30 Aura lesson
4:45 – 5:30 Mind Combat Training
6:00 – 7:00 Dinner
7:00 – 8:30 Homework
8:30 – Lights out. Mission Squad - Saving planet Soquil hook
Tuesday & Thursday
3:45 – 4:30 Aura practice
4:45 – 5:30 Mind Combat Training
6:00 – 7:00 Dinner
7:00 – 8:30 Homework
8:30 – Lights out. Mission Squad - Saving planet Soquil hook
Saturday
10:00 – 10:45 Aura practice
11:00 – 11:45 Mind Combat Training
12:00 – 1:00 Lunch
In the Afternoon we should have fun!!

And that is exactly what we did over the next couple of weeks before that official missions meeting. We worked hard, practiced even harder. And had fun chilling as a squad, knowing we had a purpose which brought us even closer together.

We were working so hard that we hardly had time to think about the upcoming all-star match. The match day was upon us in the blink of an eye. Angeleek, Brad, Evannah, Gabe and I were so excited. We had dinner and then went to get ready. We met in the dorm common room so that we could go down to the school entrance together. All of us had our 'AURA' jumpers, woolly hats, gloves and scarves. I felt very proud to be an Aura stood with the rest of my friends. I think we all felt very much a part of something special.

We met up with the others. Even though Oswald wasn't on the team he had been invited along to help Professor Dan keep an eye on us. I think he had been chosen because he was on the council and most of the team were Auras and he was the Aura prefect. There were another two lads called Chad and Otis who were Mediums. Jacob who was another Flava the year below Brad - two Audients both in year four - a girl named Mellie and a boy named Henry, which wasn't his real name but his chosen name. As like so many on WAYA his real name was a bit of a tongue twister. They were very much an item and couldn't keep their hands off each other. It was very embarrassing and awkward to be around.

Dan pulled up with the school minibus and we all scrambled inside, none of us wanting to sit next to Mellie and Henry for obvious reasons! We chatted excitedly on the way to the event, the others telling stories of the other matches they had been to. Angeleek and I just listened in not knowing what to expect but built a very good picture up in our heads by the time we got to the stadium.

Dan took us straight to our box where we were to watch the game. He then took our snack and food order and left Oswald in charge while he went to get our order. He wasn't gone that long when he reappeared with an usher helping him carry our goods. Then he pulled the infra-red goggles out of another bag. Just as we were all sorted, the commentator came on the loud speaker to let us know that the game was about to start. Everyone went silent, put on their goggles and the arena went black. Out came the two teams 'THE WAYA WARRIORS' and 'THE YANASAI YAKS'. A loud deafening cheer went up and the game commenced.

WAYA were Defending YANASAI first. The defenders were positioned at four various posts, one defender at the first post and two each at the others. The YANASAI team members went off at two minutes intervals. Each player got through the first post in no time. Player number two was at the second post just as player number one had got through. It was relentless for the two defenders at post two - but in between post two and three there were other obstacles slowing the YANASAI'S down. They had to walk over a high wire with quicksand beneath, and the wind was howling so loud and fast. If they fell off the high wire they had to drudge through the quick sand and start back at the beginning of that post - but it wasn't that simple as there were these weird creatures in the sand. They looked like a mix of a sand lizard and a shark and were really hideous.

Just as a player fell off, another player at the beginning of the post sensed it and went to help.

'Helping each other out is all well and good' I said to Angeleek with my stomach in my mouth as another member fell off into the sand, 'But what if the last player falls and there is no one left to save them from those hideous creatures?'

'Then they get eaten' said Oswald very matter of fact.

Brad laughed and explained that it rarely ever happened, but if it did then they had trained professionals and medics to go in and rescue them. Brad also said that it would mean that the game would be forfeited as not all the players would get back, and that is why their best player always went last.

Between posts three and four, it was even more gruelling. They had to paraglide across a ravine but there were pterodactyls flying around looking for a tasty snack.

'I thought they were extinct', I shouted in horror.

'Obviously not' screamed Angeleek, as one of them almost got a bite on one of the players.

'Are you two still sure this is the game for you?' Oswald asked. Him and Brad were laughing at us so hard.

'So what happens if someone gets bitten then?'

'Won't happen' said Brad.

'But if it does?' insisted Angeleek.

'They have sleeping darts' said Professor Dan 'and they are fed well before the match so they are only toying with them'.

'Ah well that's alright then' I said in a sarcastic tone. Again the others laughed at us.

I thought that getting through post four would be a piece of cake, but it appeared not. By the time the YANASAI team got there they were tired and disorientated. Their senses were all over the place and they had two defenders to navigate around. As scary as the game was, it was also so exciting, fast and exhilarating. There was so much going on and so much to see. It was the best fun, and I knew more than ever that I would love to play professionally one day.

The YANASAI YAKS got back in forty-two minutes flat and the whistle blew. There was an hour interval for the teams to rest, and I could see why - this was no football match! The teams also get a herbal tonic to pep them up and put them back on an even playing field, but the draft took about half hour to work.

We got to go in two groups to get more drinks and snacks and to look at the merchandise.

Professor Dan said 'if you want any merch, then get it now as we won't be hanging around after the game - it can take forever to get out of the carpark'.

Angeleek and I both got a programme and a Number 5 WAYA t-shirt. The player was called Nilo and he was so fit and so handsome. We read in the programme that his mother was from Earth and his father was from Soquil.

'No wonder we both fancy him' said Angeleek.

It made the second half even more interesting as we were both watching Nilo and cheering him on. The WAYA team seemed much more agile then the YANASAI team. Only one player fell in the quicksand and Nilo jumped straight in to save him. The crowd went wild and we realised we were not the only ones to fancy him. The WAYA WARRIORS got back in thirty-seven minutes and fourteen seconds. The crowd went mad. And from that day on, myself and Angeleek were firm WAYA WARRIORS supporters.

The drive back was full of excited chatter. By the time we got back to the school we were all worn out. We went back to our dorms. Angeleek and I told Addy and Alice all about it. Addy thought it sounded utterly barbaric, but Alice - as timid as she seemed, said she couldn't wait to see a match. We hugged her and showed her our T – Shirts. She also thought Nilo was to die for. We went off to bed, and I slept soundly until morning.

We were rudely awakened by Addy bashing myself and Angeleek over the head with a pillow.

'Come on you two. Alice and I have already had breakfast. If you are quick you might get a bite before chapel'.

We both yawned and stretched and slowly got out of bed. We grinned at each other knowingly and both reached for our Nilo T-Shirts. We went down to the dining hall and just managed to grab some leftovers before the kitchen shut.

After chapel, Addy told us that the missions meeting had been bought forward a few days. It was to be held at 5 o'clock in the dining hall later today. This was welcome news to both Gabe and Angeleek as they had both had another message from their nan. We also wanted to convince the council that we were *all* more than ready to go out on the upcoming mission. 5 o'clock couldn't come soon enough.

****

Chapter 8

Addy suggested that we talk to Professor Detronomy, Madam Perdido and Professor Dan before the meeting. If we could coax Madam Perdido and Professor Dan into telling Professor Detronomy how far we had come and how much work we had put in in such a short time, we may well be able to get Detronomy on board and then hopefully she could speak to Lord Raybottom and he could be the one to bring it up at the meeting.

We knew it was a long shot, but still 'nothing ventured, nothing gained'. We also decided we should have a spokesperson. We didn't want to come across too pushy and intimidating as we thought that would do us no favours. We wanted to show we could be grown up and professional, and not all talk over each other in our plight. We all decided that Addy should be this spokesperson and she agreed but only if she could have Brad as back up.

'Do you think you should tell your mother and father just in case we are successful' I said to Brad.

'I think if we tell them they will talk us out of it. They won't allow me to go, and they absolutely will not allow Flick to be a part of it. If it comes from the counsel then they won't be able to stop us - so no, I think we should just go with it and see what happens' Brad replied.

We knew that Professor Detronomy and Professor Dan would be in the dining hall at 4 o'clock as we had overheard them talking after chapel about going over strategies, so all we had to do was go and speak to Madam Perdido and ask her if she would accompany as to the dining hall as we had something we wanted to discuss with the head about our studies.

We decided that we should go down about 4.30 to give the Professors time to discuss their business. Addy suggested that Angeleek and I should go and speak to Madam Perdido now and ask her if she would accompany us.

Addy said 'Keep it simple. Lead her to believe that you want to discuss possibly moving up into year three next year and taking your exams early - and that with her help and the work you have already put in you think that you could both get this years and next years' work covered, and that you still have two terms and a bit to achieve this. We can also go in at this angle with Professor Dan, and then if they agree to this we can then make it look like they have already agreed that you four are ready to go out on a mission and then myself and Brad can show them all the data we have compiled and try and get in on the research team. As for Alice and Flick we have spoken and they don't feel ready just yet to go out on missions. They want more lessons off of Nimb. They are hoping that they will be ready by the next mission - that's if Nimb and Mikka allow Flick to continue when they find out why she is so eager to become a healer!'

Angeleek and I went off to find Madam Perdido. She was in the chapel garden sitting under a Martus tree (a cross between lotus and a passionflower - very beautiful and smelt divine). She waved at us as we approached.

'Just catching up on some reading' she said waving a copy of Wuthering Heights at us. 'The old classics are the best' she remarked. 'What can I do for you girls?'

Angeleek told her what we had discussed and Perdido's eyes lit up. She was very flattered and excited that two of her pupils were showing such promise and said that of course she would meet us at the dining hall with Professor Detronomy.

'Well that was easy' I said to Angeleek.

'Are you kidding?' said Angeleek 'That was the easy part. Perdido loves the fact she is the best teacher in the school and loves even more to show the other teachers how amazing she is. Of course she was going to go for it. It's what comes next that will be impossible. Let's hope Addy can pull it off.

We went back to the dorm to inform the others that Madam Perdido was chomping at the bit to help, even though she didn't know the full story.

At 4.30 we all met at the dining hall. I could tell that Addy was nervous about approaching the Head.

'Don't worry I have your back' Brad said having obviously noticed Addy's discomfort himself. She took a deep breath and we all entered the hall. We followed on behind Addy - she was now a girl on a mission, and suddenly seemed full of confidence. We approached the table where Madam Perdido already sat with the Professors sipping a herbal tea bought to them by Nimb. Brad glanced at his mum and smiled. I could tell he hadn't expected her to be there, but that didn't stop Addy from starting her pitch.

'May we talk with you please before the meeting starts?'

'You may' said Professor Detronomy looking slightly amused at being addressed in such a manner by an 11 year old. Before Addy could speak, Detronomy said 'So Madam Perdido has told me that you girls would like to start in year three next school year'

'Yes' we both said, which threw us a bit as we had decided to let Addy do all the talking.

Just like that - as if she felt our discomfort - Addy jumped in 'Yes they do Professor. They have been working extremely hard in both Mind Combat and Aura. They have even been having extra lessons along with Gabe and Evannah. Perdido - sorry I mean Madam Perdido - has even said that she thinks they could join Gabe and Evannah next year if they carry on the way they are going. Isn't this right Madam Perdido?

'Oh yes, very much so - they are showing real promise at being some of the finest Aura's we have had in a long time' said Perdido.

'and...', went on Addy 'both Maggie and Angeleek have managed to get in on the school team - the youngest for a long time if I'm not mistaken'. Professor Detronomy carried on sitting there with a slightly amused look on her face. 'Isn't that right Professor Dan?'

'Indeed they are' said Dan. 'The rate they are going, and the amount they practice, they will be on the all-star team before they have even left school'.

'So you see' said Addy, 'They are more than proving that they would be an asset to the upcoming...'

She was cut short by Professor Detronomy 'Mission? Hmmm, now that would be very interesting wouldn't it? If we let two first year and two third year students actually go out on a mission - albeit talented students - but very much under-prepared students. You have not even observed a mission as yet, and you think you would be an asset to the field? This is very important work our field team are taking on. A planet's survival could depend on it. What sort of operation do you think this would be to let unprepared juniors join the mission? I like the sentiment and I admire you wanting to help, which is why I invited you to join the counsel - so you could observe and learn and have a say, but there is no way I will be letting you go out on the mission'.

And before Addy could counter an argument we were dismissed.

We sat at first in the meeting all feeling a little bruised but very much wanting to know what was going on. And so within ten minutes we were participating. Addy and Brad showed them what they had compiled. We could tell that Lord Raybottom was very impressed. Gabe and Angeleek told them that they had another message from their grandmother, saying that the souls were all in limbo, that they all knew they were not ready to cross the bridge. This gave the counsel hope that once they had sorted the problem - if they could - that the healers would most definitely be able to bring the coma victims round.

This put a massive smile on both Gabe and Angeleeks faces. By the end of the meeting although feeling slightly disappointed, we all knew that this was what we wanted to be doing, and if it took a few more years to be able to go out on a mission then so be it. In the meantime, we would continue to work harder. The positive outcome was that Madam Perdido had agreed to continue giving us extra lessons to get us into the third-year next term even though she felt a little bit used by us. There were no hard feelings and Professor Dan had suggested that myself and Angeleek should move up into his third-year class straight away.

'We will have to juggle your timetable slightly, but if you take year two Aroma - which I'm told you are more than capable of by Professor Aviral, then you can attend the Year three mind combat if you wish?'

'Does the Professor think I am ready?' Angeleek said slightly shocked.

'Most definitely' said Dan. 'You are one of the top students. You might need some help from Maggie but there is no reason why not'.

'Of course we would like to' we both said.

So, in all, it wasn't as bad an outcome as it could have been. We went back to the dorm and made a pact that we would be ready by the next mission. Then we all went off to bed - not overly disappointed at the outcome, even though we had hoped it could have gone better. We all understood that we didn't want to compromise the mission and so were looking forward to learning more about our future careers behind the scenes but knowing that one day it would be a reality.

The next day at our Aura class Nimb told us that Professor Detronomy wanted to see us in her office before dinner. She also said that she thought our efforts to go out on a mission were admirable.

'Word gets about' said Addy

'Do you think that she knows Brad and Flick are members of our mission squad' I asked.

Alice looked down sheepishly and said 'I might have let it slip when I was over there. Sorry guys'

'Oh well, at least she is on our side' Addy said.

'Well she was when she thought it was just Brad. She was very proud to have both her boys on the mission, but then I kind of got carried away and said that Flick and I were hoping to go too - but that we thought maybe next year would be best. She said and I quote "over my dead body would I let Flick partake in any such thing"!'

Just before dinner we all went up to the head's office and as usual the door was open before we arrived. She invited us inside and we saw Lord Raybottom and Professor Dan sat behind a table and Gabe, Brad and Evannah already sat on chairs facing them. As soon as we were sat down, Lord Raybottom addressed the room.

'I have to say I was most impressed at the amount of data you two had compiled' he said to Brad and Addy. 'A lot of it has content that was most interesting. We are going to send the mission team out next week to assess the situation. We have some scientists we have been liaising with on Soquil and we would like you two to go with the team. We are sending an Aura with you so you won't fall behind on your lessons'.

'Oh my gosh this is huge' I thought and was so pleased for the pair of them - albeit slightly jealous.

'I have also been told by the other counsel members that you four were eager to accompany the mission team. Unfortunately, Maggie and Angeleek, although you are showing promise, we feel that the few weeks that you have been here is not sufficient enough to let you loose on the mission. The team will be back by Christmas with an update and if Professor Detronomy thinks that you are ready, I will not be opposed to the idea of allowing you to go out in the field to observe - but observe only. Gabe and Evannah you may join the team next week if you so wish, but to observe only, as you have your options next term. We think you should see how the mission team works first-hand to better enable you in your decision making'.

This was huge news it was a lot to process. But, jeez what an honour. Addy and Brad were completely made up.

Nimb was waiting for us by the dining hall doors to congratulate them and Gabe and Evannah.

'You already knew?' said Gabe

'Of course we did. Did you really think it was going unnoticed what you lot were getting up to? But I have to say we were a little disappointed that you had involved Flick'.

'And you two' she said to myself and Angeleek - 'I hope you are not disappointed. After all you have only been here ten weeks and have achieved more than most students in their whole time at the school'.

As it happened, we were not disappointed - we were very pleased with ourselves. Extra lessons from Madam Perdido and year three mind combat over the rest of the term. We knew we would prove ourselves and be more than ready by the time they went out again after Christmas.

And so, over the next week we said goodbye to Addy and Brad, Gabe and Evannah. There were lots of tears and lots of hugs, and also a sneaky party. We were also going to miss

Professor Dan. We learned we had a stand-in teacher who had in fact coached Nilo, so that was exciting, but it wasn't Dan. Myself and Angeleek put our efforts in gear to be able to join the team soon. It was in fact going to be a very productive, enlightening and interesting time. And we were determined more than ever to give it our all.

****

Chapter 9

And so that is what we did. We paid attention in our lessons, and we practiced so hard that by night time we were so tired we slept soundly.

We had our first Mind Combat match against the Flava's. It was good fun to see how the rest of the school got into it. Everyone knew that the Aura's would win - they always do. Apparently, no one is worried about coming first but the second spot is always up for grabs - but, we absolutely annihilated them.

Even their team captain said to them 'you still have to try guys'

'We are' said the team slightly exasperated.

Then we went back to practising and concentrating in lessons. Alice was very good. She kept bringing us different teas to pep us up, help us sleep, make us alert and so on. This went on for the next four weeks. On the Saturday our new mind combat coach Blake, told us he wanted to take us into town for a milkshake for all our hard work. Apparently, the teachers had said that we had been working so hard that we had forgotten to take time out for fun, and so this was what they had decided was fun for us! Don't get us wrong we really did like Blake. He had some cool stories and all, but he wasn't Dan, and we were missing our friends and Dan very much. That became apparent to us when the teachers had decided we needed this "break".

We got ourselves ready - adorned in our Aura Jumpers, hats and scarves, said goodbye to Alice and went to meet Professor Blake at the school entrance.

'You might want to go and get your coats also' he said, 'because we are going to walk in'.

We both went back upstairs together, Angeleek muttered 'You think he could have told us that earlier'. That's when I realised that we really did need to get out. We had both become a little obsessed.

I smiled at Angeleek and said 'maybe the teachers have a point'. We both laughed and decided we would have a fab time. We went back to the entrance in a new frame of mind.

We walked for about half a mile when Blake said he knew a short cut and to follow him. Just around the bend we saw a spacecraft. Brad grinned at us and winked.

'No way!' I shrieked

'Yes way - come on' said Brad.

Angeleek and I grabbed hands and ran to the craft. It was a little six-man hopper. There was the pilot, Brad, Angeleek and myself.

'Shame we couldn't have brought Alice and Flick' I said to Angeleek seeing the two empty seats. Brad just smiled to himself looking like he was the coolest teacher on the planet. I thought he still seemed like he had something up his sleeve.

'We just need to wait a few more minutes' he said practically bursting at the seams - and less than two minutes later we saw why. We were in mid conversation when the doors opened and in jumped Nilo and Chad two of the WAYA WARRIORS team. We were a little speechless.

'Oh my goodness' was all that could escape Angeleeks mouth. Mine, on the other hand just gaped wide open, so unattractive and so uncool, but I couldn't help it. I wasn't expecting that.

'Morning girls' said Nilo. 'I'm Nilo and this is my friend and teammate Chad. We hear you two are on your school team and are partial to a bit of mind combat in your spare time also. We were wondering if you would like to come and train with us today?' Angeleek grabbed my hand and squeezed so hard she left nail marks, we both just squealed.

'I take it that's a yes then' said Nilo.

We both nodded and Chad said 'take her up captain' to the pilot, and off we went. We were going to The WAYA WARIORS home ground to train with the rest of the team. I just couldn't believe it. After the initial shock we started chatting, and Nilo and Chad were very funny. We laughed a lot. The spacecraft trip alone was a treat enough to last a lifetime, but when we got to the ground and met the rest of the players and started to warm up with them, well that just exceeded any expectations ever. We were a little nervous, intimidated even to start with but we soon got into our stride and after the warmup we got to play a match.

They mixed up the first team with the second team including myself, Angeleek and even Blake. Angeleek and I were on a team with Nilo and Chad while Professor Blake was on the other team. We didn't have any really scary obstacles. We had the high-wire and the paragliding but there were no strange creatures about to take chunks out of us. The other team were brutal towards us – and we realised very quickly that they were not going to go easy on us. This made us focus all the more and our team got through in forty-two minutes.

We took a break and got the milkshake that we thought we were going out for at the beginning of the day - only it was no ordinary shake. It had a real kick to it. Both myself and Angeleek spluttered on our first mouthful - we were not expecting that. Nilo and Chad laughed at us.

'You will need to get use to that girls if you want to play professionally' Nilo said. Angeleek pulled a gagging face and we all laughed. It felt so good to laugh.

The second half, we both defended harder than we had ever done before. It was pretty tough going up against

WAYA'S finest and we were a little surprised at just how well Blake played, although why I don't know. He had after all coached most of the team at some stage in their careers.

When the last player got through, I said to Angeleek 'I think they beat us'.

'I think so too' said Angeleek - and just as the words left her lips the results came in and there was an almighty roar. We had won by two seconds. We all hugged each other and the other team congratulated us.

'Wow! what a day' I said.

'It doesn't have to be over yet' Nilo replied. 'You can come for dinner with us'.

'Can we?' I said turning to Blake.

'Of course we can' said Blake and that was that.

We went to a little restaurant that the team always uses and got a booth out the back. Nilo and Chad said that they were super impressed with Angeleek and I, and that if we carried on with the same dedication then we would defiantly make the WAYA team for sure. I felt his sincerity - I could tell he wasn't just being polite.

We both said thank you and then Blake said 'I best get these girls back otherwise the school will be sending out a search party'. We said our goodbyes to Nilo, Chad and the rest of the team, and made our way back to the spacecraft. On the journey home we thanked Blake for an amazing day and also jibed him for being on the losing team. He laughed along with us and told us he would deny it if we told the others.

We seemed to get back to the school in no time. When we got off the craft there was a car waiting for us as it was dark. We got back to the school and said thanks to Blake again and headed for the dorm to find Alice, but en-route we were stopped by Nimb.

'Hope you girls had an amazing day' she said. 'Before you go to your dorm, Professor Detronomy would like to see you in her office'.

We went straight up there. The door as usual was opened just as we arrived, and the head told us to take a seat.

'Did you girls have an enjoyable day?' she asked.

We replied 'Very much so, thank you'.

'Well hopefully this will make it even better. The mission team will be returning home tomorrow - they should be in around 9am, and we will be having a meeting at 5pm tomorrow evening in the dining hall'

'This day just couldn't get any better' I said to Angeleek, as we ran upstairs to tell Alice this news also.

We found Alice with Flick in the common room. Nimb and Professor Detronomy had let Flick come over for the day so Alice wouldn't be alone.

As we ran up to them they both said 'Have you heard? Addy, Brad and the others are returning home tomorrow'

'Well that's old news then' we both said laughing. 'My mum has said I can have a sleepover' said Flick. 'She has made us some snacks. She knows we won't sleep so we can have a midnight feast. How was your day?'.

When we told them they were so jealous but so pleased for us.

'You both deserve it' said Alice 'You have been working so hard'.

'I feel like we have been neglecting you though' I said to Alice.

'Oh not to worry, you are doing it for the greater good. Besides, me and Flick are really coming on with our herbalism, but more importantly our healing too. Flick is a really good healer. Her mum said "Who knew", and Professor Detronomy has said she will get into the school after all'

'That's fantastic news' both myself and Angeleek said.

Flick smiled and said 'Means I get to spend more time with you guys'. I secretly knew she meant Addy more.

We went to bed about 11pm with every intention of trying to get some sleep as we didn't want to be too tired when our chums came home or for the meeting. We wanted to be fresh as daisies when they told us what was happening.

But that never happened and luckily we hadn't eaten all of Nimbs snacks, because we ended up staying up until 4am. Eventually we all fell asleep and I was awoken in the morning with air being blown into my ear. I wasn't ready to open my eyes so kept pushing the source of the air away until I could stand it no longer. I opened my eyes ready to snap the window shut or whatever was bugging my poor earhole, only to find Addy loaming over me.

'OH MY GOSH!, OH MY GOSH!, OH MY GOSH!' I screeched waking the others up as I threw myself at her. 'I have missed you so much'. I suddenly had tears in my eyes. I hadn't quite realised just how much I had missed her. The others all jumped on board and hugged her too, and then Angeleek said I should go and find Gabe otherwise he will think I have forgotten him again.

Addy shouted 'Meet in the common room in half hour - tell the others'. Angeleek agreed and then was gone.

There was an awkward silence as Flick and Addy stared at each other but neither knew what to do. Then Alice broke the silence by telling Addy that Flick had found her gift.

'She is a healer and a blooming good one at that. She has got into the school next year' Addy congratulated her and they had this weird awkward hug.

I thought to myself that Alice would have to be a fool not to notice. As I looked at her, she just rolled her eyes and I knew that Flick had told her.

We went and waited for the others in the common room. I could tell that Addy was waiting to talk to us all together, so I didn't bug her with questions. I just kept stroking her annoyingly and messing about saying every two seconds 'You know what Addy? I have really, really missed you'.

After a while the others joined in and by the time the rest of the squad got there, we were rolling around on the floor while Addy was trying to fight us off, laughing like the 11-year olds we should be. It was fun. The others came and joined in for a bit until Addy was bundled so hard, she could hardly breathe. We decided then that she had had enough.

'So what's occurring then?' I said. I couldn't wait any longer - the suspense was killing me.

'Well...' began Addy. 'The science behind it will bore you so I'll keep it brief'.

And she went on to explain what was happening to Soquil. She got two plastic bottles to demonstrate.

'Soquil has two ozone layers around it - one that rotates clockwise, the other anticlockwise. There is a small tear in each layer, and as they reach each other, the force of the ozone causes suction on the layers, and as they pass, the force rips the tears further'.

She squeezed the two bottles at the same time with the necks of the bottles touching, causing the bottles to suck together, then moving them apart to show the impact of the air escaping.

'This is serious' I said. We could all make sense off what she was showing us. 'So what are they doing about it then?'

'That's for Gabe and Evannah to explain' said Addy. 'That is their field of expertise'. I looked at her admiringly. She even sounded like a professional.

'I'll keep it brief' said Gabe taking the reins, 'as it will all be explained at the meeting...but basically, we have to go in and repair the outer layer first. That will stop the immediate danger. It will then mean that the healers can jump in and do their bit while we are mending the middle'.

'And they think they can save everyone?' said Angeleek.

'Oh definitely' said Gabe ruffling her hair.

'And how are they going to fix these layers' I said. 'And what has caused it to happen in the first place? Will they be able to stop it from happening again?'

'Wow! lots of questions Maggie. One at a time' said Gabe.

'But yes...' said Addy 'They can definitely stop it from happening again. It will be a case of re-educating the inhabitants on how to look after their planet. A team will be staying behind after the mission to help them set up a programme.'

'They will need lots of healers on hand and I heard them say you two will be ready by then' Brad said to Alice and Flick.

'Wow! Really' they both said 'How exciting'

'And what does mother think of that?' said Flick.

'She is really excited. You won't be going in until it is safe, and she will be with you. She said it will be a real family outing'. They both laughed.

'And? How are they going to fix it?' I said.

'I think it will be better to wait until the meeting. They can explain it better. But for now, just know that it can be done'.

And that had to be enough information until 5pm.

****

CHAPTER 10

'So, what's been happening here then?' Addy asked.

'They stuffed the Flava's in the mind combat' Flick said. Everyone laughed.

'So we heard little sister' said Brad.

'How come you guys know so much?' asked Angeleek,

'Our teacher has been filling us in' said Addy. 'You'll love her guys. She is the cutest little thing ever - she is like a pixie. She is from Yona which is also where Lord Raybottom is from. Apparently whatever height they reach at the age of twelve is the height they will stay for the rest of their lives. So diddy bless them. Anyway, her name is Professor Trixie, and she has been telling us all the gossip. She is good friends with Perdido and Nimb, and Perdido and Nimb have been keeping an eye on you lot and filling us in'.

'Well they could have done the same for us' I said.

'They are not allowed - it's protocol. They can't talk about anything in case things are overheard' .

'That's fair enough I suppose' I said, although I was still slightly miffed.

We all went off to the chapel. I was looking forward to having a chat with my grandad today. I had so much to tell him. He always put things into perspective in a way I could see clearly. I loved that man so much when he was alive, and the fact I was getting to be with him now was truly a blessing.

After the chapel we went to the dining hall for our feast and today they pulled out all the stops, unbeknown to the rest of the pupils it was for the mission team, but they had no idea. We feasted and chatted until we were all talked out.

After the feast, Dan came over to say Hi, and wondered why myself and Angeleek were not practicing our mind combat. We started to explain and he chuckled saying 'relax guys, I'm messing with you, but I do hear that you went and played at the WAYA ground. I suppose Blake is your new favourite coach'.

'Never could be Professor Dan, but we are touched that you think you have competition!'.

He walked off laughing to himself. Everyone was back and it felt right. I couldn't wait until 5pm. I was getting slightly antsy. Addy sensed this and came to sit with me.

'Why are you so prickly?' she asked gently

'I'm not sure. I guess I just want to know what is happening - I never use to be so impatient. I think me and Angeleek have been working so hard, and you guys got to go on the mission and Brad said that they will be needing Alice and Flick, and I guess I'm just being silly'.

'Oh you think that you two won't be coming with us when we go back!? You can stop that nonsense. They have already been talking about you guys and how much you will contribute to the team'

'oh', I said, feeling a bit daft but very much relieved.

'Yes - oh' said Addy.

It was a brisk day but the sun was out so we decided the eight of us would take a walk.

'Hold up' we heard Dan say. He had Nimb, Mikka and Joe with him. 'Mind if we join you?'

'Not at all' we all said and so we all took a stroll.

Dan and Mikka had been very good friends at school and still were. They were telling us stories that had us in fits. Nimb said they were always in trouble, and if she didn't keep a close eye on them they still would be!

'Life is about the fun times too. You have a few weeks before the next mission trip. Make sure you guys build memories that are not all to do with saving planets. Climb trees, take a boat out on the lake, get into mischief, just take the time for fun also - otherwise you will burn out. This was my worry about you lot being allowed on the mission's team in the first place, but I have to agree with the Professors. You can't let talent like yours go to waste, but please promise that you won't miss out on being kids'

It felt kind of nice being lectured by Nimb. It felt warm and motherly.

Later when we were back in the dorm, Brad apologised for his mum's outburst.

'Don't be silly' said Angeleek. 'It felt like a piece of home'.

'Here here' I said, and the others agreed.

We went down to the hall for the missions meeting at 5pm. Most of the team were already there. There was a heated discussion going on when we entered between Professor Detronomy, Lord Raybottom and Nimb. When they saw us they stopped abruptly. Lord Raybottom acknowledged us and went and took his place at the head of the table. He welcomed the counsel and then started the meeting.

'Firstly' he said, 'I'd like to start by welcoming the team back'. We all clapped. 'What they have found out Is most interesting and also solvable. It has been interesting having the young members on board - their input has been insightful. It has shown us even more that we must always keep a fresh pair of eyes on the task in hand'. He looked at

Nimb and she was glaring back at him. 'Once the outer crust has been repaired, the healers can start to heal the coma victims, and the research team are already putting a programme together to help the planet start an educational programme to help the inhabitants keep their planet healthy. They know what has happened and so are very much on board with helping save their planet. They know the consequences if they don't stick to their regime - Once a tear has been fixed it will always remain fragile and any further tearing to that site will not be fixable'.

'So, the first task is to get this outer crust repaired. Because this tear was a result of the middle crust it should be a relatively easy fix, albeit slightly dangerous. Extreme care should be taken with safety lines and equipment to ensure nobody gets sucked out into space. Dan, Mikka, Joe and Ivan will start on this as soon as they return. That side of the island has already been evacuated and so we are not planning on going back out until after Christmas. Instead they are going to make sure they all know exactly what they are doing - given the data that Addy, Brad and the science team have gathered we can recreate a mock of what has happened and practice on that. Dan will announce his team later. We need all the healers we can get on board and Nimb and Mikka have very kindly agreed to letting Flick join us. We are aware she is not yet a member at the school, but we need all the healers we can get. Thank you to both of you'.

Nimb was still glaring at him. I knew it wasn't about Flick as Brad had already said she was pleased, but you could cut the tension with a knife.

'Once the outer crust is secure' continued Raybottom, 'and the healers and researchers can get on with their jobs, there is the task of fixing the middle crust. This is going to be very tricky and could take some time. The planet spins inside the two axis and creates a very strong suction as it spins on the damaged side of the planet, hence why the outer tear. We are going to need a crew to ensure this fix runs smoothly. We are going to need fit and nimble bodies'.

I could start to see where this was going and why Nimb was so cross - after all, she already had one son on the team and Brad was only a third year.

'They are just children' Nimb said venomously.

'Very capable children' Lord Raybottom said. Mikka was holding Nimbs hands, I could tell that he was in agreement with Lord Raybottom but that he was feeling his wife's anxiety. 'These "children" will be given more training than anyone has ever had before with all the new technology we have now and the data that two "Children" have already compiled. Yes it won't be easy but the danger is minimal, and they are no ordinary children. They have the ability to follow instructions, work as part of a team, and trust that what they are being instructed to do is the right thing - no questions asked. They will go through a four-week training programme with lifelike simulations, and if they don't feel like they are ready, they can walk away. Now I will hear no more on it.'

After Lord Raybottom had done he's speech, he said that the research team was still on Soquil and that Addy and Brad would be joining them again when the team went back out. They were needed here to help Dan with the simulations the research team had put together. He then went on to ask Nimb if she would head up the healers. This sort of softened the blow a bit but I could tell that Nimb was still cross. And then he said that Dan would be talking to the members he wanted on his team. Individually.

Dan headed over to our table. I thought he was going to speak to Gabe and Evannah and I was waiting for fireworks to erupt, but he addressed me and Angeleek.

'So you two are causing quite a stir' he said rubbing his temples. 'Lord Raybottom wants me to ask you guys if you will come on the mission with us, and Professor Detronomy thinks it is also a good idea'.

'But you and Nimb don't want us to go' I said slightly confused and also hurt. The others were going - even Alice. *And* Flick. Who wasn't even at the school yet.

'It's not that we don't want you to go' said Nimb gently. 'You see, it's that Lord Raybottom thinks you should actually help on the mission, not just observe'

'Oh' said me and Angeleek.

'So, how do *you* feel about that?' asked Nimb.

'Um well, I personally think that we are more than ready', I said. 'We have been practicing hard. We even played a match with the WAYA WARRIORS and our team won. Our senses are really developing fast. Ask Madam Perdido.'

'And what about you Angeleek?'

'Um. Well the same as Maggie just said, although I am a little nervous'.

'Nervous is a good thing' said Dan 'I wouldn't want a member of my team going in without a few butterflies'.

'So when do we start training?' I said.

'First thing tomorrow' said Dan 'Most of the training covers a lot of your lessons, so you will just need to revise. Your teachers will send your coursework up to you, so you won't fall behind.'

'OK cool. And Nimb, please don't worry. I'm sure Professor Detronomy wouldn't let us go if she didn't think we were ready'.

'Professor Detronomy see's you as the talent you are' said Nimb. 'What she and Lord Raybottom are not seeing is the fact that you are still children. Just promise me one thing. Every Saturday, take the time out for fun?'

'We will. And we will make sure the rest of the squad do also'.

And that was that. We were on the team - eight adults, two thirteen-year olds and two eleven-year olds. The youngest ever. They had had all age groups healing before, but Addy and Blake were also the youngest researchers too. We all felt very proud of ourselves.

As a goodwill gesture to Nimb, the eight of us went outside. Me and Alice had decided we needed to teach the others how to play rounders. I also thought Addy could do with the exercise as she always had her head stuck in a book. She agreed to join in saying the Hall of Minds could wait until tomorrow.

So, we explained the game and then me and Alice picked a player at a time. I chose Addy first and Alice chose Angeleek. Fair play - I got the worst player and Alice went for who would probably be one of the better players. I had Gabe and Evannah on my side which left Blake and Flick for Alice.

We went in field first. Then Nimb bought us out a big jug of some herbal juice she had been working on. It was delicious, and made us all so happy with no care in the world. Just eight friends having a game of rounders making the most of the evening before it became too cold to go outside.

It was our turn to bat. Alice's team had got 16 rounders, so we knew what we had to beat. I went first and got a rounder, followed by Evannah who also got a rounder. Then it was Gabe's turn. He got around to third stump, and when Addy stepped up, you could see the other team thinking this is going to be easy. Alice bowled the ball and – whack. Addy smashed that ball so far. We all cheered as Gabe got home and all laughed as Addy ran to first stop then decided it was too much effort and walked the rest of the stops - still before the ball made it anywhere near the last stop. Wow we had a powerhouse on our team.

'Bad luck' I mouthed to Alice.

We won by 4 rounders. 20 – 16. Not a bad day if I do say so myself. It was good fun, and we all went up to the dorms laughing and decided that that should be our Sunday evening game.

****

Chapter 11

Next morning after breakfast we met in an old disused classroom. As far as the rest of our classmates were concerned we were having extra lessons as we were going to be moving up a few years at the start of January and so needed the extra help. Nimb was also out on loan to us. The classroom was a bit dusty and unloved, so before the rest of the group got there we took some time to clean it up. It looked pretty spotless by the time Dan arrived.

'Wow!' he said. 'You lot have been busy. We need to go and get some things from the other parts of the old school. I need five desks, a chalkboard, rubber, chalk - get as many different colours as you can find, a projector and pens. Again grab an assortment of colours and a big table to hold Addy and Brads model. Whatever you can't get we will have to beg, borrow or even steal from one of the other classrooms' he said with a cheeky chuckle. I did love Dan he was so funny.

Addy wrote us a list and we all paired up. I went with my girl Addy. I hadn't seen much of her lately and wanted to hog her. Call me selfish but I wanted her to myself.

When we were out of earshot of the others, I asked her how things were between her and Flick.

'It still feels awkward' she said.

'Do you think that's because you are trying to keep your feelings a secret' I suggested

'Perhaps' said Addy.

'Well, I think everyone knows. I haven't said anything, but Nimb sensed it the day you guys imprinted. She must have told Mikka. Brad obviously knows - I have seen the way he watches the pair of you. He always has an amused look on his face. I know Alice knows - I think Flick must have told her. The only one I don't think knows anything is Angeleek. I think you should tell her and then get to know Flick a little better. She is very funny, doesn't seem to take anything too seriously. She has calmed down while doing her healing but other than that she is a right little livewire.'

'Wow!' said Addy. 'You know more about her than I do'

'Yes' I said. 'So you better get on with it, before the universe thinks it has made a mistake' I chuckled.

We had fun collecting all the things for our new classroom. Every now and then we would bump into another pair, rifling the same cupboard as us. It became a bit of a game. We managed to get some chalks off of Angeleek and Gabe and they chased us down the corridor. We only got away because Professor Meridet came out of her classroom. We were supposed to be being discreet as we didn't want anyone walking in on our mission training and then finding out that Soquil was in trouble.

When we were almost done, we went into one of the classrooms that had some old desks and bumped into Alice and Flick.

I ran up to Alice as she was picking up a desk and said 'Hey let me help you with that' then I turned and poked my tongue out at Addy and smiled. She shook her head and smiled back. Me and Alice left the room.

When we were out of earshot Alice said 'subtle – much!' and laughed.

'Well it needed to happen' I said

'I'm with you there. Flick has been driving me nuts' Alice agreed.

By the time we got back to the classroom it was nearly lunch time and our classroom was looking loved and homely. Nimb had bought in her herb garden trough and some plants and we even had some new curtains up at the windows that Nimb had been working on. Professor Dan told us we might as well go early and be back early, as there was no point in starting on anything now. He said that we could go straight to the kitchen and they would feed us there, as we would probably be having different sittings to the rest of the school.

So, we all piled out and headed straight for the kitchen. It was hungry work lugging furniture around and trying to remain inconspicuous.

As we were walking down the corridor Brad caught up with us and said 'about time' nodding in the direction of Addy and Flick, who were both in deep conversation. I could tell they were enjoying themselves as Addy was constantly laughing and Flick was being even more dramatic in her storytelling to get such a reaction from Addy. It was lovely to see.

'What's with them two?' Angeleek said catching up with us. We all laughed and rolled our eyes. 'Oh' she said. 'I thought as much but I didn't like to say anything. Would have been nice to have been told' she said.

'Oh Angeleek, are you upset?'

'Of course not' she said. 'How could anyone be? Look at them they are adorable'.

After we had filled our bellies we headed back to our new classroom. Dan had managed to get a couple of sofas and a coffee table, and Addy and Brads model had been brought in.

Professor Dan said 'from now on - inside these four walls I want you to call me Dan. Addy, Brad - if you wouldn't mind setting up your model please, and Nimb you can take Alice and Flick over to the sofas'.

Nimb had the girls healing plants and said that if any of us get a headache, toothache or any such pain, the girls could practice on us. Later when Nimb felt they were ready she was going to take them to Waya general hospital. She had okayed it for them to practice on some of the willing.

Addy and Brad were busy putting their model together that was a prototype of the simulation they had set up at the counsel headquarters. Once myself, Angeleek, Gabe and Evannah knew exactly what we were doing, we would then go to headquarters to practice on the simulation. Dan had some tasks for us to accomplish leading up to this.

Once Addy and Brad had set up their prototype, we gathered around the table and they explained what it is we will be doing. Dan showed us the instruments we would be using and what they were for. He explained that this will be done in the dark with the wind howling past us while we were strapped to safety harnesses, so we had to make sure we knew what we were doing. Anything we didn't understand, he and Addy and Brad would explain. 'Even if it took a hundred times' he said. 'Even if everyone else has got it but you are not quite sure, you need to shout out. If you are not 100% sure you could endanger the mission and even get yourself or someone else killed. We have four weeks until we leave and another two weeks until you will be expected to do anything, as only myself, Mikka, Joe and Ivan will be repairing the outer crust. Any questions so far?'.

Gabe and Angeleek both wanted to know, when they got to Soquil would they start to remember their parents? Would they have the feelings for them that they used to have before

Waya had supressed them? They both felt very much attached to their nan now since they had been in communication with her. They were worried that if their feelings did return that this would jeopardise the mission as their minds would not be fully on the job.

Dan explained that the feelings and memories only started to return when they were in contact with that person, and as they wouldn't have any contact - this wouldn't be an issue.

'But what about our nan?' Gabe asked. 'We have grown quite close to her, and while I was observing you guys at the last trip I couldn't stop thinking about her'.

Nimb had overheard this conversation and said 'We can take you both to see her while the outer crust is being repaired, and then when you are happy that everything is ok I can give you a herbal draft that will help you focus on the job at hand. We can try the draft when you go and use the simulator. If you feel this is not going to work then you don't have to join in on the mission. This has to be your decision.'

Gabe and Angeleek seemed content with that response. And so, Dan passed the reins over to Addy and Brad to talk us through their prototype.

What Addy and Brad had come up with was truly spectacular.

'You guys did this by yourselves?' I asked.

'Indeed they did' said Dan proudly. 'It has saved us a lot of valuable time and resources. The counsel are highly impressed with them, and when Lord Raybottom told them about you guys, this prototype, and the simulation that they also helped build, is what swung it for you guys'

'Wow! you two, well done' I said admiringly.

The prototype was a replica of what was happening to Soquil. They had built the planet on its two axis showing the holes in both layers. I could see how they thought that fixing the outer one was achievable, albeit dangerous, as they would potentially be hanging out - just chilling in space as you do!

But the middle one! I looked over at Addy while she was explaining what we would have to be doing and I had a slight suspicion that even she was not entirely convinced that it would be that easy. Brad explained again what was happening, but it was even more clear looking at their model, and he demonstrated how we would be doing the fix. We would have to be manipulating the energies back together, but the force of the spinning looked like it would be totally impossible.

'Don't worry yourselves too much' he said. 'Wait until you see what we have made for you at headquarters. I don't want to focus on that yet as you still have to be at the top of your game. Dan will be giving you challenges to do - similar to the things you get up to in mind combat classes, but with some danger thrown in just for fun' he laughed. 'This will help you focus and then when you are ready, hopefully within the next 10 days...'

'10 days - no pressure', I said to Angeleek under my breath.

'...We can get you up to headquarters' Brad continued, 'to try all the cool stuff out up there. You are going to love it.'

So, that is what we got up to over the following days. Alice and Flick healed everything that moved, plant or person. One day I had the worse headache and I asked Nimb for a tonic, but she said 'Oh no dear. You don't need a tonic. Come sit, girls. Maggie's head needs healing', and in no time - just like that I felt better. Better than better even.

Addy and Brad helped Dan explain to us the science behind the mission, and while Dan was putting the rest of us through our paces, they were in the Hall of Minds gathering even more information. They preferred the Hall of Minds to the library as they said the greatest minds were there. Every book that ever mattered was either written by someone who had passed over and was willing to explain to them, or one of the great minds had read a book that might have had some useful information in it that they would share. It cut down on all the reading time.

And as for Myself, Angeleek, Gabe and Evannah - when we weren't being wowed by Addy and Brads brilliant minds, we were off training mind combat harder than ever. Dan was throwing some real nasties at us. He was using a lot of gale-force winds as he said this was what it was going to be like out on the mission.

We stuck true to our words and took Saturday as a 'chill day' to just have fun and 'build happy memories' as Nimb put it, and we played rounders again on Sunday. We still couldn't get over how good Addy was at batting. Dan, Mikka, Joe and Ivan joined in, partly for fun and partly because Dan said it will help with teambuilding for the mission.

We worked hard and looked forward to our Saturday and our rounders on Sunday evening, and by day 11 - one day later than Brad had suggested, we were ready to go out to headquarters to start training in the simulator.

****

Chapter 12

Dan picked us up in the school minibus along with Mikka and Joe. Ivan was going to meet us there as he didn't live too far from headquarters. We chatted about mindless stuff on the way there.

As we approached the security gates Addy took mine and Angeleeks hands and said 'I can't wait for you to see what we have been working on. You will be blown away'. Gabe and Evannah smiled to themselves.

'You two know don't you?' I asked.

'Sort of' said Gabe.

'We saw at the end of the last mission, but we didn't get to try anything out' said Evannah. 'But I have to say, I am so excited'.

'Me too' said Gabe.

We pulled up outside the hanger where we thought the equipment must be, but when we got inside we all stood in the middle of the room and then the ground started to move.

'Hold on' said Dan, and the ground went down rapidly about 50ft underground.

'You really should have handrails' I said quite out of breath. I was even more out of breath when I saw the room we had been deposited in. There were all sorts of gadgets and gizmos.

'I think Addy and Brad should explain some of the things to you four while myself, Mikka and Joe go and let the counsel know we are here and find Ivan" said Dan. 'We also have some things to discuss with Lord Raybottom, so knock your socks off but be sensible.'

'As if you even need to tell us that', Addy said. I could tell she was a little hurt.

'I'm not talking to you Addy' he said, and nodded in the direction of myself and Gabe. We were practically chomping at the bit to get to all this cool stuff'

'Oh' said Addy. 'I see what you mean. Don't worry Dan - we won't let no harm come to them'.

'I think we should start with your suits first' said Brad.

'I'll help you into them' said Addy. 'So, we have made them of the lightest fabric. We have used a mesh material so that they will be warm, breathable and flexible. They also have a spring in them so every movement will be a little quicker than you are used to. Go take them for a wander. You can use the training ground'.

We went outside and then Addy and Brad engaged the suits.

'Ok' they said over the tannoy 'You are now in "suit mode" so be careful'.

We went for a little stroll around the ground. It took a little getting used to. Evannah looked like Bambi on ice to start with - and I couldn't help but chuckle. She went to hit me playfully and as I went to dodge her, I fell over as I myself wasn't entirely used to the suit either. Everyone laughed including Addy and Brad from their control room.

'That will teach you for laughing at her' said Brad.

I got myself back up, slowly this time and carried on walking around the grounds.

'When you feel ready' said Brad, 'take them for a run'.

We all ran around the grounds. It was amazing. It felt like we were running on air and at least triple the speed we could normally run. When we were all doing this with ease Addy called us back in. They had a pot of Nimbs tea on the brew.

'You might want this. It will settle your stomachs. In a bit the motion will catch up with you".

They weren't kidding. I felt like I was going to be sick, and Angeleek actually was.

'Oh my goodness' she said. 'Will that happen every time?'

'Only to start with - until you get used to it...and you *will* get used to it. Don't worry' said Addy feeling sorry for Angeleek. 'Here' she said. 'Drink this tea'.

She gave us all the tea and we started to feel better in no time.

'Right' said Brad. 'Are you ready for the cool part?'

'What? You mean that wasn't the cool part?' I said.

'Oh no, you just wait for this. It will blow your mind' said Addy, and they came out with helmets.

'These are designed so we can talk to you and guide you if need be. if you come across any matter you are unsure of, we can tell you how to move forward. But - better than that, they are in sync with your minds, so be careful when taking them for a spin. You thought the suits were fast? Well, combined with these bad boys, your reflexes will be lightning speed. Do you think you are ready?'

'I think I'll sit this out for a while' Angeleek said. 'You can all demonstrate for me' she laughed.

Evannah said 'If you don't mind, I think I will sit this out also. I think I need a little more time with the suit'

'That's cool' said Addy.

'Just me and you then' Gabe said to me with a grin.

I was a little apprehensive, but I went out into the ground and put the helmet on.

'Right. Thumbs up when you guys are ready', Brads voice was saying - this time into our ears via the helmet.

'Only the left ear is working' I shouted.

'No need to shout Maggie. We can hear you just fine' said Addy.

'You almost popped the speaker' came Angeleeks voice as if she was inside my helmet too.

'We only need your left ear as that is the side of your brain that takes in information. Right, thumbs up when you are ready'.

We both put our thumbs up.

'Now take the babies for a stroll'.

It seemed like before we even thought about putting one-foot in front of the other the suits were already on it.

'You will get used to it' said Addy. 'Just go with it - let it take you. You almost don't even have to move your limbs. Just think about what you want to do and your suit will do it automatically. Once you relax into it you will find that you can just sit back and use your senses only'.

it was a really weird and surreal feeling but it was also extremely cool.

'I think I want to go back in in my suit only' I heard Evannah say, and next minute she was there beside me.

Then we heard Dans voice 'How are they getting on?'

'Better than expected' said Brad, super excited at seeing his and Addy's invention come to life.

'You not feeling it Angeleek?'

'I just felt really sick' she said. 'But that looks so much fun. I just don't think I'm ready to throw up again at the moment'. She sounded deflated.

'Here' I heard Mikka say. 'Nimb made these tablets in case any of you got motion sickness. Try this, and then give the suit another go'

'Thanks' said Angeleek sounding more upbeat.

We all knew to trust in Nimbs lotions and potions by now.

'Just give it a few minutes to kick in' he said, and before long Angeleek was back in her suit running circles around me and Gabe who were still trying to get to grips with the lightening reflexes of the suits.

We heard Dan say to get another pot of that tea brewing so they can have it as soon as they come out. Then he said 'Five more minutes guys. Then you can go and grab some lunch'.

We came into the control room, had our tea, chatted for a bit while it took effect - and then went and grabbed some lunch. Dan showed us where the canteen was and then said he was going to join Mikka, Joe and Ivan for a play with the suits.

'Be back in an hour' he said, and then we watched as he skipped off excitedly. You could tell he really did love this invention.

'You two are amazing' I said.

'You really think so?' said Addy.

'Are you kidding? That was the best ever'.

Her and Brad were grinning ear to ear. We ate our lunch and chatted excitedly. We couldn't wait to get back to it - so we all decided to cut our lunch short. We got into the control room and the others obviously hadn't heard us. They were such a sight. They were doing summersaults and pulling some really bizarre shapes.

Brad said 'I'm sorry guys I can't resist this. Here Addy. Press record on the camera when I play this music'.

He played the music in the control room only, so that Dan and co couldn't hear it and Addy recorded them. It was hilarious. When they came into the room, we all acted as if nothing had occurred. We had agreed we would play it next time Nimb, Alice and Flick were with us.

We put our suits back on and carried on practicing. It didn't take long for Angeleek and Evannah to join us with the helmets. We had such a fun day.

'Tomorrow' Dan said, 'we will do some mind combat with them on'.

'Fantastic' we all agreed, and went back to the school in time to do some homework, which actually wasn't that bad as Dan had said that apart from romping around in suits, we were doing way more advanced stuff than the others were doing. It was just a case of writing the theory behind it, which Addy helped us with.

We were in the dorm when Alice walked in with Flick.

'What are you doing about school now then?' I asked Flick.

'Professor Detronomy has told my school he wants me here full time now" replied Flick. 'But I am underage to board, so I still have to go home with my mum after dinner. Speaking of which I am starving.'

We all piled down to the dining hall and ate hearty meals.

'I hope they have space cakes for pudding tonight' said Addy. 'My brain is going into overdrive. I really need to relax before bed'.

We all agreed with her.

'I'm not allowed the space cakes either' said Flick. 'Until I'm eleven - which is only three weeks' time'

'Then we will have a space cake party' said Alice.

'We can convince mum and Professor Detronomy to let you have a sleepover again' said Brad.

'That would be cool' Flick smiled at her brother.

I couldn't help thinking how cool it would be to have been born on Waya and not to have to give your family up. Alice squeezed my hand and I smiled at her as I could tell she felt the same. It wasn't as bad for Addy or Angeleek because they had their siblings here, but myself and Alice were alone. Even though we were all one big happy family and even though Nimb was a very good mother figure, it wasn't quite the same. But on Waya you couldn't stay melancholy for long.

Brad and Flick convinced their mum and dad to let Flick stay with us for a while

'Preferably until lights out please?' said Flick.

'Nice try' said Mikka. 'You can stay until 8 o'clock. Me and your father need to discuss some business with professor Detronomy and Dan anyway. Be in the school entrance by eight. No later young lady, otherwise we won't trust you again'.

'Thanks mum. Thanks dad' Flick said hugging her parents.

And then we all went off to the dorm together. We found a quiet spot and told Alice and Flick all about our day.

'That sounds so cool' they both said.

Then told us what they had been up to. Apparently, Nimb had gathered some of her friends from the neighbourhood with various ailments and let the girls loose on them.

'One of them smelt like mouldy cheese and had whiskers on her chin' said Flick.

'Yum - attractive' said Addy.

'Yes very' laughed Flick. They really were starting to bounce off of each other.

'Anyway' said Flick. 'She kept saying she felt no better, which was a lie as I knew that what I was doing was no different to what I had done to the others. It felt the same to me, and I could no longer feel her pain - so I know she was lying. Anyway, I made her pay for it. I gave her back what she had and then some!!'

'FLICK!' Alice gasped. We all just laughed.

'Good girl' said Brad. 'That's my sister'. And then she said goodbye to us.

Brad and Addy walked her down to their parents.

Addy told me later that when Brad and her were walking back to the dorm Brad had said 'I'm so glad she has you. We thought she was going to fall off the rails. She has always been a little bit of a handful, but since she has met you she has calmed right down. Her healing is really coming on. My mum and dad don't think she would have ever discovered it had it not been that she was trying to impress you'.

'That is lovely Addy' I said, and we both hugged. I could feel she was so complete and so happy, it was contagious.

****

Chapter 13

The next day I woke early. I couldn't wait to get back into them suits. I got out of bed and noticed that Addy's bed was empty. Maybe she had gone down to breakfast early, I thought and so I dressed and went down to the dining hall. But she wasn't there. I grabbed something to eat anyway, and then went to find her.

I finally caught up with her coming out of the hall of minds. She looked so deep in thought she hadn't even noticed me until I took her hand.

'Oh hi' she said shocked and almost guilty.

'What are you up to?' I said looking at her suspiciously. 'This is the second time I've caught you coming out of there lost in thought'.

'Oh, um I don't know what you mean' Addy said slightly concerned. She could tell I wasn't going to drop this, but before I could push Flick came bouncing up to us.

'Where are the others?' she said.

'In the dining hall I suspect'

'Mmm food' she said rubbing her tummy - not that there was anything to rub. She was so tiny.

'You are as bad as Addy for food' I chuckled.

They both seemed to like the fact that they were alike in that respect. I mouthed at Addy that we weren't done. She mouthed back 'OK later - when we get back before dinner. Meet me at the hall of minds'

'What are you two whispering about' said Flick.

'Nosey Parker' said Addy and they both laughed.

We all met up in the entrance again and Dan pulled up in the minibus. He said to jump in and that Mikka and Ivan were going to meet us there - they had things to do. We were all so excited.

We pulled up at the bunker. This time I was ready for the floor to move and it wasn't quite as bad. When we got into the room Dan said to "knock our socks off" and that he would be back by lunchtime with the others so they could have a play while we were at lunch. We all looked at each other and chuckled under our breath. He said that after lunch when we were all ready we would have a Mind combat match - myself, Angeleek, Gabe and Evannah versus Dan, Mikka, Joe and Ivan.

'So you better be up to the challenge' he chuckled leaving the room.

'Right challenge accepted' I said. 'You better both be on our side' I said to the Addy and Brad.

'I think I'll be on dad's side' said Brad.

'Traitor' said Addy poking her tongue out at him.

We practiced hard and when Evannah and Angeleek were ready we even had a go with the lights out just using our senses. This actually made it even easier for me as I felt like I was now part of my suit. It was a little surreal but we were in sync with each other. I just sat back and thought all my moves through and the suit just did it for me. It saved me having to think about my physical self - I could just concentrate on my surroundings and how my physical being was going to navigate around the obstacles we had set up for each other. I felt like I was floating like Nimb and Professor Detronomy.

It only seemed like we had been at it for 2 seconds when I heard Dan's voice saying "five more minutes" to us.

'Are you sure?' I said. 'I think you lot just want to hog the space. You are worried we will beat you later'.

Dan laughed and said 'stop being so cheeky'.

We came back in, had our tea and then headed down to the cafeteria.

'You were like nothing I had ever seen out there' Addy said.

'What do you mean?' I asked.

'You were mesmerising - like you and your suit were doing a ballet performance. You were so peaceful and moved with grace and precision, I almost cried. You exceeded my expectations for the suit.'

'I have to say, I do feel like when I have the suit on it is an extension of me' I replied 'Like we really are one and the same. Does that sound weird?'

'No, not at all, that is what we were hoping for - but with you it is different somehow, I can't explain it'

'Well what do the others look like then?'

'Like they are wearing suits that are enhancing their abilities'

'And I don't look like that?'

'No. You look like you are putting an extension of yourself on. It will be interesting to watch later'.

We had our lunch and, like the day before we couldn't wait to get back to it so we headed back early. We snuck into the room so we could have a laugh at the others prancing about, but they were not in there.

'Hey you guys' we heard Lord Raybottom.

'Hi' we all said.

'You're a bit early. We are setting up your tournament. You four better disappear - we don't want the others thinking you have had an advantage. You two can stay and help' he said to Brad and Addy.

I looked at Addy and put my fist in my mouth as if I was scared. She laughed. She knew I was far from it. She could tell I was pumped and ready to give the older lot a run for their money.

'Give us fifteen minutes' Lord Raybottom said.

And so we went off to find the competition. They were sat in the courtyard just chilling. They looked so relaxed. If only they knew, I thought to myself. I had this inner belief that I could take them on by myself and still come out victorious. Having the other three was just a bonus. Obviously, I wouldn't say that out loud as I didn't want to sound conceited, but that is just how I felt. We had some banter with the guys and then all went back into the bunker. They were ready for us. A lot of the other counsel members had heard what was going on and had come along with their infra-red goggles to hand. This just made me even more hungry to get this show on the road. I never used to be this competitive on Earth, but since finding out I was an Aura, I just seemed to have this power from within that my senses were so sharp. And with Addy and Brads suit, well I was the full version of me.

'OK' Lord Raybottom said over the tannoy 'Let's see what the fuss is all about. Brad is going to be on the men's side and Addy the Ladies'.

'Hey' said Gabe, and everyone just laughed.

'OK, let the battle commence'.

We played tag in the dark with obstacles in the way. We all just tried to get to the other side while also stopping the others from getting to their side. It was weird that we thought that the suits seemed super-fast yesterday. Now I felt like everything was in slow motion. I could see all the other players moves before they even took them - and we beat the others hands down.

When the lights went up there was applause around the bunker. Lord Raybottom, said that Addy and Brads invention was like nothing else, but they couldn't get over how mesmerising I was. I told Brad to video us just messing about because I didn't know what I was doing differently, and when I watched it back I could see what they meant.

'Wow' was all I could say.

'Wow indeed' said Dan. 'We didn't stand a chance. Remind me to be on your team next time'

'The ladies did well didn't they' said Gabe.

Then we all packed up and went back to the school.

I hadn't forgotten about Addy and the Hall of Minds, and when we got back to the school I said to the others that we would meet them at dinner. Me and Addy had some business to attend to.

She rolled her eyes and said 'I was kinda hoping that you had forgot'

'No such luck' I said.

'OK' she said, 'but you can't tell the others and you must promise me that you won't do what I have done'. She was deadly serious and wouldn't let me through the doors until I promised.

'OK, OK I promise' I said, although what could be that bad?

When we were inside, Addy explained that it wasn't just a "Hall of others Minds" but that it was also a "Hall of your own Mind".

'Eh?' I said.

Addy shook her head. 'We do things in this life because of how we lived in previous lives, and sometimes this is a good thing and sometimes it is a bad thing. I just wanted to iron out my bad kinks "as it were" so that I could be the best possible version of myself, without having to iron out the kinks as I went. I wanted to see what they were and be on top of them. I didn't want to waste my life'.

'OK' I said. 'Sounds perfectly normal to me. So, what is your problem?'

'I just wanted you to know that this is why I was doing this and for no other reason'

'OK'

'Well I discovered something about me and Flick and it kind of bothered me, so now I'm obsessing over it'.

'Oh' I said. 'But you do know you and Flick are meant to be together right? There can't be anything that bad?'

'Well actually there is. Come - but be quiet. I don't think our age group is supposed to be in here', and she pulled me into a room. It was set out like an old cinema room, but we were the only two in here.

'Are you ready?' said Addy.

'Yep. I think so' I said.

'Then sit back and watch the lives of Addy and Flick'.

The screen fired up, just like an old-fashioned cinema. The film took a while to warm up, and then on to the screen came this very attractive girl. I could tell it was Addy by the eyes. But that was all that was the same. She looked like she came from a very privileged background. She looked like she was getting ready for a ball. She descended the stairs and at the bottom was a very handsome Flick, only this time she was a boy - but again you could tell it was her by the eyes and the way he held himself. They were a couple and it was a very strong love that they shared. It was like watching your favourite chick flick. They were so much in love but then he went to battle and never came home. It was so sad. This girl version of Addy lived out the rest of her life alone. No one was ever going to match up to her handsome man, and she died in old age of a broken heart.

They met again in another life. Again, Addy was the girl and Flick the boy. They were deliriously happy in this life too albeit they were very poor, and before his 24th birthday the boy version of Flick contracted cholera and again died, leaving a heartbroken wife behind. Again she lived a full life but never remarried as who could ever match up?...And again she died in old age of a broken heart.

The third life - Addy was the man and very handsome too. He was a very powerful businessman with an amazing brain. All he did was work. And then one day this beautiful little thing got into the same lift as him and that was that. They were destined to be together forever. But again, an illness took the male version of Addy this time. It was the other Flick that had to live out her life without the other part of her. It was such a sad tale. This went on for two more lives.

'Oh my gosh Addy, that is so tragic but so awfully romantic. You two are so supposed to be together'

'Romantic, romantic' Addy butted in. 'What are you on about romantic? Can't you see the pattern? One of us is going to die young and leave the other one heartbroken!! How can this be romantic? This is our lives! I need to find a way to stop this from happening, or at least - if I can't stop it then I need to make it so that it is me that dies. She is so full of life. I couldn't let it be her if I can do something about it - but then I would be leaving her heartbroken. Can't you see that this a big ugly mess?' she threw her head into her hands and began to cry.

'But why do you have to fix anything?' I asked 'It's your time to be together now'. I couldn't understand why she was so upset. They had been together for five lifetimes and it had ended in tragedy and now they finally get to be together. What was her problem? Then it dawned on me that my brainy friend had not spotted the pattern.

'Oh Addy' I sighed. 'You poor thing. How long have you been fretting over this?'.

'Since before we went out on the last mission. I couldn't wait to get back so I could try and figure something out. I nearly decided not to have anything to do with her, but you've seen her. She is just so loveable and cute.'

'Oh Addy, Addy, Addy. You haven't spotted the pattern have you?'

'Of course, I have. One of us is going to die young'.

'No Addy - you're not' she looked at me dumbfounded as if she couldn't believe that I had watched the same thing as her. 'Don't you see? This time you are both girls'.

The penny dropped, and she cried so hard she shook.

'My poor brainy girl' I said stroking her hair, and when she stopped crying, we went and joined the others for dinner.

Addy was so smiley. Her and Flick were having a ball, laughing at each other's jokes and just loving life. I only hoped my deductions were correct. I also didn't know if I could keep my promise to her and not go and have a look at my previous lives. But for now, I was just enjoying being with my friends. Tomorrow was another day.

****

Chapter 14

And so it was, we went to HQ again and did some more practice in our suits. Dan said there was no point looking at anything else today as it was Friday and so the weekend was upon us. We had lunch, and then went back to school early. Then we went and joined Alice and Flick in our classroom and knuckled down to some theory. A couple of hours in, the door opened and in walked the rest of the crew with cake and treats and some juice all made by Nimb.

'We thought you had been working so hard you all deserved a little treat'.

We packed our stuff away while Nimb set up the table with her buffet and then we all got stuck in.

'This is delicious Nimb' I said with a mouthful. The others all agreed.

'My wife is amazing isn't she?' smiled Mikka. You could tell he really did love her. I wondered if they were twin flames also, and Nimb turned to me and nodded. I smiled to myself,

I really needed to learn how to keep my thoughts guarded. They could get me into trouble one day.

After we finished eating Brad said, 'Myself and Addy discovered something the other day. Can we run it by you guys?'

'Well son, we are supposed to be having a couple of hours off' said Mika.

'This won't take five minutes' he insisted, and so it was agreed. He winked at Addy and she put her hand to her mouth and chuckled, and then it dawned on me that they were about to show the video of Dan, Mikka, Joe and Ivan pulling shapes in their suits. I nudged Angeleek. She looked at me and smiled. She was already on it.

'We were in the bunker just running through some alterations to one of our probes when we saw this. It was quite alarming and very disturbing'

'Not for the faint hearted' Addy added.

The others looked concerned and then Brad pressed play. We were all in bits. Nimb and Flick were laughing so hard I thought they might pass out. This was the first time that Nimb, Flick and Alice had seen this. And of course, Dan, Mikka, Joe and Ivan had no clue that we had caught them in the act. They also found it hilarious although I did get the impression that Ivan was slightly embarrassed and wasn't used to being the butt of anyone's jokes. One thing he was going to have to get used to - after all, we are kids at the end of the day.

As we were leaving the classroom and as we had eaten early, Nimb packed up the rest of the buffet and told us to take it to our dorms for later as we probably would be too full for dinner. Flick was able to stay over being as it was the weekend. Mikka also told us that we should grab breakfast early and meet them in the school entrance at 9:30. They were going to take us into the city.

'Oh wow, thanks' we all chimed, and went off to the dorm.

We didn't really do much - just chilled and chatted. Flick said that she had heard there was going to be snow at some point over the weekend, so we better wrap up warm tomorrow.

'Wow snow' I said. 'Can you remember the last time we saw snow' I asked Alice. Alice shook her head

'No actually I don't'.

'We get it every winter on Waya' said Brad. 'We get all the seasons that the rest of your planets get. Autumn, winter, spring and summer. Your planets are all similar in that respect. That's why they are habitable. But we get the weather pure because Waya isn't polluted'.

'I hope it does snow' said Alice, 'I do like to build snow people, and make snow angels'.

'Snow people?, snow angels?' Gabe laughed. 'If we get snow we are defiantly having a snowball fight - boys verses girls'.

'Um, I think not' said Brad. 'After the stunt we just pulled, I think my dad will be wanting to get his own back. I think it will be us versus them'.

'Even better' said Gabe. 'We can go in hard'.

I was really looking forward to tomorrow.

We got up early and adorned our school jumpers. Alice lent Flick a jumper as they were close in size, met the boys in the common room and went down to breakfast. When we got to the school entrance, Professor Detronomy was waiting for us.

'Ah' she said. 'I'm glad you are with this motley crew Flick. Do you all mind just coming to my office before your trip? It won't take long'.

So we all followed her.

'Don't worry' she said. 'The others know you are with me, so they won't think you are running late'.

When we got to her office she said to take a seat. I couldn't help thinking that this sounded official.

'Yes it is rather official' the Professor said to me. Damn I'd done it again. Addy never had her thoughts listened in on. I would have to ask her to help me with it later.

'Lord Raybottom asked me to give you all these' she said passing us little brown envelopes. 'Now you are part of the mission team and you are giving so much of your valuable time and still making time for your schoolwork we all decided that it would be only fair that you got a pay packet like everyone else. It would again be appreciated if you didn't discuss this with the other students. It will only lead to them wanting to know why. But I'm sure I didn't need to say that to you all'.

'Wow, thanks' we all said. I think we were all taken aback by this. Professor Detronomy showed us out of her office and told us to enjoy our day.

'Wow, this is amazing' said Gabe. 'It is amazing being a part of the team, but to get paid for it as well - well result'.

We all agreed. We met the others and Dan said we will take the hovercraft.

'This day just keeps getting better' said Angeleek. And off we went to the city.

There was so much to see. The boys decided that they should meet us for lunch as they didn't want to be dragged around girly shopping and so Mikka said to meet at 'The Veg Bar' at 1pm. Apparently it was "the" place to go and eat, and us girls went off to look around the shops. It wasn't like Earth here on Waya. There wasn't the need for consumerism. You bought what you needed - it was just a given. If you wanted it but didn't need it, it stayed in the shop window. But it was still good to look. We did get some cool stuff, and we all went to the salon and got our hair cut. This was a treat that I hadn't missed - but was thrilled to be getting done. Then we went and met the boys.

'Nice haircut' Dan said to us.

I did like Dan. He always noticed the little things. He really was a nice guy.

As we sat eating and chatting, Flick suddenly squealed making me jump out of my skin.

'Look?' she said pointing out of the window. It was snowing.

'Better hurry up and finish this lot' said Mikka. 'It comes in thick and fast here on Waya'.

We finished our food and all went back to the hovercraft pronto.

'It will be really thick by the time we get back to the school' said Dan

'I feel a snowball fight coming on' said Joe. 'What do you think dad? Us against them. Get them back for being so cheeky yesterday'

'Oh yes most definitely' said Dan.

Brad looked at us and winked. He had already called that one.

'Bring it on' said Gabe. He was so up for it.

'Oh no' Alice said. 'I feel we are going to get very wet'.

'Warm baths for everyone later then' said Evannah.

When we got back, they didn't even give us a chance to go and put our things back in our dorms.

'Oh no you don't' said Joe when we reached into the back to grab our purchases, and that was that. We were bombarded. No holds barred. They played dirty - so we played dirtier. Alice was gasping next to me after taking a snowball to the face.

'All I wanted to do was make snow angels and build snowmen she sighed'.

Brad was getting Joe back for the assault on her. We snuck off early to get first bath.

Evannah saw us and caught up with us. 'Wow that was fun, but do they even know the meaning of gentle?'

We all laughed and went to the bathrooms. I had brought a really thick dressing gown and fluffy slippers in town after they had told me how cold it was going to get, and after my warm bath it felt really nice slipping into it.

The next day we went for breakfast then went to chapel. I had a good conversation with my grandfather, telling him everything we had been up to. He said he was very proud of me. This choked me up a little. We had our feast and then the boys decided they were going out for round two in the snow. We said we would give it a miss and then when they were out of sight we went out the back entrance and went and made snowmen and snow angels. Flick thought it would be fun to fill a bucket with snowballs and get the boys from the top of the tower. We all thought this was a fab idea.

We dragged our buckets to the top and launched the balls over the top. The boys couldn't see where it was coming from. Every time they looked up we ducked. We laughed and laughed.

Then we dried off and warmed up and went to the counsel meeting. After the meeting Nimb asked us if we wanted to spend Christmas at theirs. It was a few weeks away but she wanted to make sure she had enough food for us. She said we could have a think about it.

'What's to think about?' I said. 'I'd love too. Thank you', and the others agreed.

So that was that. We went to HQ Monday to Friday lunchtime. We always finished early on a Friday.

The rest of Addy and Brad's inventions were mind-blowing. I could see why Lord Raybottom was so thrilled by them. He himself was also a closet geek. We had fun at the weekends, and then it was the Christmas hols. We were all more than ready for the mission and were actually looking forward to a bit of a break before we left. Most of us were shocked at how many people had gone home for the Christmas break. At least three quarters of the school were from Waya. Brad explained that gifts were more prevalent in families, and as

96% of people on Waya acknowledged their gifts - it was understandable that the school was made up of Waya-ens. I hadn't thought of it like that.

We packed our bags after breakfast and went off to Mikka and Nimbs. Their house was amazing. We were there for the whole week and played games, laughed, and just all round had a lovely time.

On Christmas day, the whole team turned up. We spoke about the upcoming mission and ate and sang and played more games. We all just got one present each. Nimb had said that here on Waya they only do a "Secret Santa", as Christmas is all about spending time with your family and friends - and again, here on Waya they didn't buy wasteful things. Those of us that were not used to this actually thought it made sense. We had had such a lovely time with everyone, that the secret Santa was just an added bit of fun.

Christmas ended all too soon, and before we knew it we were being briefed about the mission. And just like that we were in the spacecraft and off we went. We were apprehensive, but more than ready to take on our first mission.

It took 3 months to get to Soquil, although we were unaware of this as we went into sleeping pods. And then one day the pods opened, and we woke up on Soquil. We stepped outside. The view was breath-taking.

'You might think this is nice' said Dan, 'but you wait until you get to the affected part of the island. Just to warn you – it's not pretty'.

'How does it feel to be home you guys?' Mikka said to Angeleek and Gabe.

'Strange' said Gabe.

'Do you still think you are up for the task?' asked Dan?

'Even more so' said Angeleek, and Gabe agreed.

We got into a hopper and headed over to the East of the planet. Dan wasn't wrong - it wasn't a pretty sight. I felt Angeleek recoil next to me.

'Right' said Dan 'Let's get this show on the road'.

****

Chapter 15

We went to HQ on Soquil and met the guys we would be working with, and our teacher Professor Trixie who would be helping us keep up to date with our studies. We were then shown around our living quarters where we dropped our stuff off and were taken to the canteen. We were told to help ourselves to anything we wanted, and if they didn't have what we wanted to speak to the chef and he would be only too pleased to make whatever we wanted. He was used to all cuisines.

We were then told to meet at the training station at 2pm. Addy, Brad, Gabe and Evannah knew where it was and so we were left to our own devices for a couple of hours. We chatted about the mission and Addy told us about last time they were here - and the others chimed in with their own stories.

Then we went to the training station.

'Ah good you are here' Dan said. 'Tomorrow myself, Mikka, Joe and Ivan are going out to the outer crust. I would like you guys to practice in the simulator for the middle layer until it becomes second nature - until it becomes muscle memory, because nothing is going to prepare you for the mental side of it. If you know what you are doing to the letter then hopefully the rest will be manageable. While you are not doing that we think it would be a good idea to watch our mission so you can take away some pointers and see how best you think you might react under the same circumstances. You can then take them into the simulator with you and practice some more. Also don't forget to study. I wouldn't want you to get back from Soquil and fail your exams. If you do, you might not be able to come on future missions. Addy and Brad can run through any of the technical stuff you don't understand so you would be wise to pay attention to them, after all - these inventions are their babies. They know them best. Good luck guys. Have a quick practice and then head to your living quarters for some rest and then get some sleep. Tomorrow will be the beginning of a gruelling few weeks.'

We stayed and had a practice for a bit and then all went off to our bunks.

When we got back to the living quarters we really took in the room. It was large and spacious and the walls to two sides were floor to ceiling glass.

'The views would have been stunning before this' Angeleek said sadly.

'They will be again' I tried to reassure her.

'Yes they will be' said Gabe 'although I'm not sure how long it will take for all the vegetation to grow back'.

We were then disturbed by a knock at the door. It was Professor Trixie just checking in to make sure we had everything we needed and to let Gabe and Angeleek know that she had arranged for them to go with Nimb to see their grandmother tomorrow if they wanted too.

After she left I turned to Addy and said 'Oh my goodness, she is so adorable. She reminds me of the fairy Tinkerbell'.

Addy looked a little baffled.

'She is a fictional fairy from a children's book by J M Barrie which was later made into a film called 'Peter Pan'.

'Ah OK. I'll give it a read when the mission is over. I'm sure I'll be able to find it in the library' she said.

We all just chilled and chatted for a bit and then decided that we should get an early night. The sleeping pods were amazing. They moulded to your body and made you feel like you were sleeping on air.

'I think these are just for the mission' Angeleek said, 'I think I would have remembered sleeping in comfort like this'.

'I think they were designed here for the astronauts' said Addy. 'They really are quite up on their technology here on Soquil'.

Angeleek smiled to think that her planet was so far advanced. She pulled her sheet over her and said 'This is heaven. Even the sheets make you feel like they are part of your skin and just the right temperature.'

'Yes they are cool' said Addy. 'If the temperature in the room drops, the pods warm up to keep your body at a nice temperature for sleep. In the morning they drop a few degrees gradually so you wake up gradually. Like I said the technology is very impressive.' And with that we all fell asleep.

As Addy had said, we woke up gradually in the morning. I stretched and yawned

'Wow that was the best night sleep I have had in a long time' I said.

Then we met the rest of the squad for breakfast. We learned that Dan and the others were on their way to the outer crust. We rushed our breakfast and went up to the viewing tower to watch them.

'They will be at least another three hours before they can even start anything' said one of the senior technicians from Soquil. She said welcome back to Addy and Brad.

Addy said 'You might as well get into your suits'.

The other technician eyed us suspiciously and said 'They really do train you guys young don't they'.

We got into our suits and headed for the simulator. It was set up to mimic the middle layer. We had tools in hand that Addy and Brad had demonstrated to us on Waya and we went about our mission. We were like a tag team, and we were precise. We were missing two other members, but we managed.

When Dan and the rest came back from the outer layer they were going to take a couple of days break, and then they were going to come out with us in two's on alternate days, so the fact that we had completed the first phase of the mission by the time Addy called us in was pretty good going. We got out of our suits, hung them up and then went to the tower.

'That was amazing you guys' said Brad. 'That tech that was in here earlier was super impressed. She even got a couple of others in to watch you'.

'Glad I didn't know we had an audience' said Evannah. 'It was scary enough out there'.

'Where has she gone?' I said.

'To get us some food' said Addy. 'The others are nearly ready to start the first phase of their mission. We thought you might like to watch - but don't get any food over the controls. They will be out there for about two hours'.

'Then when they are on the return trip we can do some homework' said Brad.

'Oh joy' said Gabe.

The technician came back with an array of food and introduced herself as Jane, which wasn't her real name but was easier to pronounce.

'You guys looked good out there' she said. 'Thanks so much for coming out to help us'. She seemed warmer and friendlier then when she first met us. Maybe she didn't think we were up for the challenge.

Addy explained that Soquil was very similar to Earth and the other planets that were habitable in the way that the ozone worked.

'Take Earth for example' she said, 'where 90% of the ozone layer was around 15 - 30km above the Earth's surface - in the stratosphere. As opposed to about 93% of the ozone layer on Soquil which is around 40km above the surface – also in the stratosphere'.

This would be where we would be doing our part. Dan and the team were another 5km up. Unlike Earth and Yanasai, Soquil had this upper section above the stratosphere that circled the middle section. It was all very technical. Brad and Addy were always blowing my mind with the stuff they knew.

It was really interesting watching Dan and the team. They worked so fluidly together.

'They have been doing this a long time together' said Brad. 'They know each other inside out, which really helps as they don't have to use up excess energy communicating. It's tiring enough out there'.

There was definitely a lot we could learn from them. I got a pen and paper and started making notes. Rather than the others doing the same, we all had an input as to what we thought we could do to make our next go in the simulator better.

'Not a lot' Jane said. 'You guys flow so seamlessly already'.

'Yes but there is always room for improvement' I said.

'And practice makes perfect' said Angeleek.

'Well' said Jane, 'You are a bunch of perfectionists. No wonder you are so good'.

'Can't afford not to be' said Gabe. 'After all this isn't child's play' he said smiling at the irony of his statement.

The lads had finished for the day and were heading back down. Addy was chatting to them. They were pleased with how well it had gone and said they thought they might be done in a couple of days. That made it feel so real - that we would be out there in just a couple of days. it was insane, but I was confident. This was what we had trained for.

Dan and the others met us in the cafeteria after they had freshened up.

'It wasn't as bad as we thought out there', said Mikka. 'The harnesses and suits make easy work of it for us. You two really have done a good job'.

'Wish we had had these on other missions' said Ivan.

Addy and Brad were feeling chuffed with themselves.

After we had finished eating, Dan suggested we leave it an hour and then meet for a swim. The pool was surrounded by glass sides and bottom and was over the top of what would have been a ravine.

'It apparently was spectacular swimming over here when the planet was thriving' he said. 'It would be nice to come back when the vegetation has grown back. We never get to see these different planets at their best'. He sounded a little sad at this.

'Why don't you do it sometime then?' I asked. 'Take a trip around to some of the places you have been to?'

'I wish we could' he said, 'but only the scientists and a few authorities know what we do, so to come back is virtually impossible'.

'That is so sad' I said. 'I bet this would be stunning when it's at its best'.

'It is' said Angeleek. 'We have an infinity pool at my grandmother's house'.

'How is your grandmother?' I said.

'She looks peaceful. And Nimb said there is no question of a doubt that they can heal them. So that's good. Just can't wait for that part of the mission.'

'Well if the lads are finished in a couple of days you won't have too much longer to wait'.

The next day was pretty much the same as the first. The lads came back and said they would definitely be finished by the next day. We had six phases to our mission and we had only gone over three of them. We would get another two in by tomorrow but we would then be doing the sixth phase cold.

'It won't be cold' said Joe. 'You have gone over it enough on Waya, and the sixth phase is just finishing off - so no real biggy. The real fix will have been done by then. It will be reinforcing the mesh'.

'If you say so' said Gabe.

'Trust me buddy, these suits are amazing, and when the hole is secure you won't have any other obstacles in your way. Like I say it will just be a case of securing it'.

Gabe still seemed not too convinced, but I could see where Joe was coming from. Maybe it was because it wasn't my planet that was in danger.

Dan was right and by the end of the next day, the first part of the mission had been a success. Now the healers could start their part.

'First thing in the morning' Nimb was saying to Angeleek, who was keen for them to start straight away.

And the next morning Alice and Flick were nowhere to be seen. Mikka said at breakfast that they were up and out early. There were ten healers and over a hundred patients. He said that Nimb was hoping they could all heal two each a day, and that Nimb herself was going to work on Gabe and Angeleeks grandmother.

'She should be sat up in her bed by lunchtime and if you two are not too tired you can briefly visit her. We will let you know while you are out on mission when she comes round. So go out there and don't worry about a thing. Do it for your grandmother' he said.

****

Chapter 16

The team went up after breakfast. It took an hour to get there. We suited up twenty minutes before and when we arrived, we put on our helmets.

'Welcome to your first mission' said Brad in a very dramatic way. It made us all laugh.

'On a serious note' came Addy's voice, 'don't get the equipment out yet. Just have a little float around - get yourselves used to it. Apparently, it can feel unusual the first time'.

This was a good idea as it didn't feel anything like the simulator. Although it didn't take long at all to get used to. We went back to the spacecraft and got our mesh. The space crew let us down one at a time at our various different places around the hole which was the size of a football field. The suits were equipped for us to get to exactly where we needed to be. As we got closer you could feel the suction of the hole.

'Wow that is really strong' said Angeleek, fighting against the pull of the hole and finding it hard to breath'.

'Just relax with your breathing Angeleek' said Brad. 'The suits are equipped to adjust. You are just hyperventilating now'.

I flicked my speaker to Angeleek to reassure her that we were all breathing fine now, and also the pull didn't seem as strong. Just as I thought that, Brad explained that it was part to do with our suits adjusting and part to do with the spin of the outer layer.

'The suits can't quite adjust fast enough because the movement is too quick. You should be alright for another hour. We will let you know when the pull is coming around again so you can prepare yourselves'.

The mesh was amazing stuff. It was light and thin, but in the shape of a bees honeycomb. The idea was to layer it over the middle layer, quite far back from the hole but leaving some overlapping the layer. Then the gases will entwine around the mesh. We were to build it up like this in sections always going around the hole. The mesh was like a spider's web and when in place was actually very strong. We worked like little honey bees quite successfully and then Addy's voice came into our helmets telling us that the outer layer was on its way back around and to brace ourselves.

It didn't feel as bad this time - probably because we were used to it now and it was very windy up there anyway, but when I looked over at Evannah next to me, part of her mesh was being torn away again - not as bad as it was initially but still not very secure. I flicked my switch to tell her but Brad was already on it.

'Don't worry the rest of you. You need to still keep working at your part. If Evannah hasn't got a hold on it by the time the next lot of mesh is due to go on then we will have to use another lot of mesh over the top of it. That must be where the tear started.

We continued to work like this until our mesh was secure. Evannah was still struggling though and getting tired when the next pull from the outer crust came around. I could see her struggling so I said to Brad and Addy that mine was secure and that I would go and help.

Brad said 'You can't Maggie. You are in the wrong position. Evannah's got this'.

Evannah was sounding breathless in the tannoy and said 'Guys, I don't think I do. My arms are just so tired. The pull is so strong'.

'Why don't we all go back up then?' I said. 'And then I can go down in her position - give her a break'.

'Good idea' said Addy. 'Are the rest of you ready to come up?'

'Yes' they all said. 'All secure'. And then the team above winched us back in.

When we got back in, myself and Evannah swapped positions. She was physically shaking.

'Be careful Maggie' she said. 'You are already tired and it is strong out there'.

She wasn't kidding. The G force was powerful.

'Wow' I said to Brad and Addy. 'That is strong'.

'Yes' they both agreed. 'We will have to put you, Angeleek or Gabe in that position tomorrow'.

I worked away as best I could. I had taken down another lot of mesh, but as the pull came around again I could feel it giving a bit.

'This is insane. If we leave it like this, it will be back to square one by the morning' I said 'and it could start to weaken the parts either side of it. The gap is still too wide. The air is pulling through too much. I think we are going to have to do the next lot'

'We can't' said Brad. 'The spacecraft hasn't got enough solar power in it for you to do that and get you back'.

'Aren't Dan and Mikka coming up?'

'They were going to but we told them that you lot were coping fine. That was before Evannah's started to give way again. They decided to give it a miss until tomorrow.'

'Well you will have to go and get them. Then the spacecraft can go back with Evannah. If I hold this here can't you see the tension that its under?'

'Oh my gosh, yes' said Addy. 'I see what you mean! Brad go and tell Dan, and arrange another craft'.

I heard Brad saying the craft will take another hour to get up there and it would be cutting it fine for the other craft to get back.

'Well, we have to do something' continued Addy. 'Look at the readings'.

Just as Brad was agreeing Dan came into the control room. 'I was just coming in to see how the guys were doing' he said, 'and I sensed something was wrong'.

When he saw the readings, he said we will have to take a light spacecraft. We can carry enough power for the other craft to get back and just have enough juice in ours to finish the next layer and get us back.

'We will be with you guys in an hour or so. Hang tight' he said.

I was winched back up to the craft, and the others said that we could start on the next layer now. When Dan and Mikka get here we can tag team with them to do that part.

'It does need two people on it. You need one either end. The force is strong when that outer crust whips around. You did really well Evannah'.

'I'm sorry guys, but I don't think I will be able to go back out there today. Even with the suit I am physically drained'

'We thought that. That is why we said you can go back with this craft when the other one gets here.'

I had a cup of Nimbs tonic. The others had already had theirs...then we went back down for round two.

'When the other craft arrives, you will have to be careful while they do the changeover of your harnesses' said Brad. 'It might be safer if you come back in for that'.

'That will just waste time' I said. 'Surely they can swap them over from up there?'

'We'll just have to wait, and see what Dan and Mikka suggest then. But Maggie, what they say goes. You must listen to them. They have been doing this for years'.

'Of course I will listen' I said, feeling quite hurt.

But Brad was right I was getting carried away, the adrenalin was pumping so fast. You don't get the adrenalin in the simulator in the same way.

By the time Dan and Mikka had arrived we were nearly done with the second section - all apart from the section we were struggling with. They radioed that they were coming down and that myself and Gabe should remain where we were until they got there to hold our sections in place. They said that Angeleek might as well come up now. They also said that she could go back with Evannah as there was no point in her hanging around. The only reason myself and Gabe didn't get to go back was because the craft couldn't hang around for too much longer as it was already tight on getting back.

We said a brief goodbye to the girls as Dan and Mikka were being winched down. They got to the section just as another pull came around.

'My, that is strong' said Mikka. 'It's almost as strong as the outer crust. Are you two OK to put some extra webbing on the sides while we do the back'.

We were both starting to feel the strain of the day but agreed. We could do it until the next pull came around and then we were done for the day.

'That's fair enough' said Dan, 'and well done for saying so. Some people would carry on and put themselves in danger'.

We stayed until after the next pull and then were winched up. We had some more of Nimbs tonic and then just chilled watching Dan and Mikka on the monitor, and chatted to Brad and Addy. Then we heard Trixie's voice.

'Hi Gabe, just thought you might like to know your nan is awake. She is doing fine. You and Angeleek can go and see her when you get back. I'll pack your dinner so you can eat it on the way to the hospital, I'm sure you are very tired.'

'Oh wow, that's amazing news' said Gabe. I could tell he was a little choked up. I reached out for his hand and smiled. 'And thanks for letting me know Trixie. Does Angeleek know?'

'Yes, she does. She was very happy - so happy she cried' said Trixie.

'That figures' said Gabe. 'See you in about two hours' he said checking the clock.

When Dan and Mikka were back on the craft and we were heading home they suggested a meeting. Addy went and got Angeleek, Evannah, Joe and Ivan.

When they were back, Dan said 'good work today guys. That was tough going. If we had known it was going to be like that we would have sent a craft out sooner. Sorry guys'.

We all agreed that there was nothing to apologise for. It hadn't been picked up on the Beaufort meter, so how could they have known?

'Anyway', said Dan. 'We have decided that Joe and Ivan will go up with you tomorrow. It is going to take two on that section again. The closer we get to the middle, the smaller the hole - so the section after that should be ok. We can have one person on the craft and tag team it. We think that Evannah had the worst of it today and Maggie towards the end so we are thinking if Gabe can tag team with Ivan and Joe on that section and Maggie and Evannah can swap between the one opposite giving them a bit of a breather. Is that OK with everyone?'

We all agreed it was, although Evannah did say she was feeling really tired and that her limbs were aching.

'That's OK. Joe can you take the girls for a massage, and then some of Nimbs recovery tonic should do it. If everyone is happy then I think we can call it a day'.

Angeleek and Evannah said their goodbyes.

When it was just the four of us, Dan said 'you two should make the use of a massage when you get back. It really does help'.

Gabe said 'I am going straight to see my nan when I get back. Trixie said she would box me up some dinner so I can get straight off'.

'OK then we will send the masseuse up to your room. Just let me know when you are heading back. You will appreciate it - trust me buddy'.

Gabe thanked him. Then we flew the rest of the way back in silence wrapped up in our own thoughts.

****

Chapter 17

The next morning Evannah wasn't feeling it - partly because she was still aching but also it had spooked her a little.

'That's OK' I said. 'I didn't get the worst of it like Evannah. I'm sure if I stay at the opposite end to the section that was giving us grief yesterday, I will be just fine'.

So it was agreed that Evannah would sit today out. She said that she would have another go in the simulator and watch the mission from the control room with Brad and Addy, and maybe get another massage - and that she would be fine for tomorrow.

We had breakfast and then took off. Ivan said it should be easier today because we knew what to expect, and because a good section of the hole had been secured.

'That's if your section is still intact' said Gabe.

'Don't even joke' said Joe. 'We've been on missions before where we had wished we had pulled an all-nighter'.

When we got out there it was quite the opposite.

'Oh my gosh you guys, are you getting this' I said excitedly. The hole was rapidly repairing itself around the mesh. In fact, just like Brad and Addy had said would happen, eventually you wouldn't be able to see the mesh, and it would one day just dissolve under the natural gasses. Well that was already happening.

'What do you think we should do?' I asked.

'I think we should go back on board and call a meeting' said Ivan. 'Can you guys call the others?' he said to Addy and Brad.

While they were doing that, we were being winched back up to the spacecraft. By the time we got up there the others were already in the control room.

'So what's the verdict' said Mikka. Ivan explained the situation.

'What do you guys think' Dan was saying to Addy, Brad and Jane?

'Well' said Addy. 'We had expected this to happen once the mesh was in place, but we didn't expect it to happen straight away. We thought it would take six months, a year maybe for the full effect. Mother nature really is a wonderful thing'

'So what? Do we just leave it? How long will it take to completely heal?'

'Well' said Brad. 'I think if we left it, and the habitants were not allowed back, then maybe three months to fully repair, but I also think that being as we are here we might as well finish the job. That way the planet can start repairing itself, the vegetation will grow back, the inhabitants can move back and the planet will hopefully continue with its low emissions and use ozone friendly products to stop this from happening again'

'They have already seen the devastation' said Jane, 'and the government has put measures in place. I'm with Brad. Finish the job so our planet can start growing back'.

'OK. Are you guys alright with that?' Dan said to us. We all agreed that we thought it was a good idea.

I said 'Maybe we don't have to be as rigid as we were yesterday. Maybe we could get it done today. It will be a long day again, but maybe Dan and Mikka can come up tomorrow and see how it is looking?'

'Yep. We'll go along with that said Dan and Mikka. 'What do you guys think?' Dan was saying to Addy, Brad and Jane.

'Sounds like a plan' said Addy.

So, we were winched back down into position, mesh in tow. There was still a suction on the left side where Ivan and Joe were working, but nowhere near as bad as yesterday. We didn't overlap the mesh like yesterday either -we went to the edges. We went around once, and then went up for a break.

Addy told us that they were sending another craft up and that Evannah was on it. As it would only take four people to do this next bit, Joe had said that he would go back down until she got here and then he would go back with Ivan. There was no point in everyone being up there. We had some of Nimb's tea and then got suited up.

The next section was going great guns and we were half way done by the time Evannah got there. Joe and Evannah swapped over and within half hour we were going back up for another rest. We really were taking things a lot easier today after yesterday, and it was actually fun - and whilst we were out there it was kind of peaceful.

It didn't need the four of us on the last little bit. We would be bumping into each other, so Angeleek said she would stay on board. We went back down and had quite a fun time. We were all talking to each other - Addy and Brad included. We were upbeat about completing our first mission. I said to the others that I wouldn't mind seeing what Nimb, Alice and Flick were doing - see if I might be able to develop my healing as I knew I could do it. This would be a perfect opportunity to try it out, so long as I didn't get in the way. Evannah said she would quite like to try it also, so we decided when we got back that we would ask Nimb.

It didn't take us to much longer to finish up and before we knew it we were back on the craft and heading back to HQ.

We got back just in time to have dinner with the others. We were all in high spirits at how well it had ended up going and then Nimb, Alice and Flick walked in. We told them all about it and then asked how they were getting on.

'We are a little behind' said Nimb, 'but not greatly. Some of them are taking longer to find their way back'.

Myself and Evannah told them that we wouldn't mind tagging along tomorrow and Nimb thought that would be a good idea. Alice and Flick were also pleased as they said that the other healers were all old! We laughed and said maybe you can give us some pointers later. They agreed and we finished our dinner, and everyone was tired so we all retired to our rooms.

After showers, and when we were all ready for bed, Alice and Flick started showing us a few things. Angeleek said it looked interesting and decided to join us.

'The boys won't know what to do with themselves tomorrow' I said. Addy cleared her throat next to me in a very dramatic way. 'And you of course' I said hugging her.

'Well actually me and Brad are helping Jane go through some papers for the government, telling them what laws they need to put in place'

'Ooooh check you out. That's very official' we laughed.

And then decided it really was time for bed. I could not wait for my pod. These things were amazing, and we were an hour early going to bed - and we were going to get an hour lay in as well. Ahhh bliss.

Next morning, when we went down to breakfast, Gabe had decided to come with us.

He said 'Mikka is driving you lot over so I'm going to tag along and see nan. She is supposed to be coming out today. We are going to take her back with us for a bit and spend a bit of time with her before she goes off to my mum and dads. Mikka will be bringing us back lunchtime and you lot can come back later with Nimb.

When we got to the hospital, I could see what the girls meant. All the other healers were old. I thought Flick was just being her usual cheeky self and they were really going to be Nimbs age, but these ladies were old! Flick came running up to us when she saw us. She had just finished bringing someone round.

She said 'Why don't you come with me Maggie'.

I was just about to join her when Nimb came over and said, 'you girls can shadow us for a bit and then we will let you do a group healing on one of the patients that we will be starting on tomorrow. You can spend an hour with each of us and see how we all work differently, feel how our energies manipulate the patients energies. Come - I think you will like it. It is actually quite therapeutic. Maggie, you can come with me first. Angeleek you can join Alice and Evannah. Well good luck with Flick, my little live wire'.

Flick wrinkled her nose up at her mum, and then walked off with Evannah. I looked over and saw a big smile reach Alice's lips when she saw Angeleek. She must have really been missing her friend, and good old Nimb could obviously sense it.

It was very interesting working with Nimb. She was so informative and her energy was so powerful. Looking around the room at the other healers was a sight. The colours that were emanating them and mingling with their patient's bodies were truly beautiful. Although some of the patients that had only just started receiving their healings – well, their auras were very murky.

Nimb saw the direction I was looking in.

'It can be very draining to start with, but as the healing goes on and their energies start to respond you get this nice glow' she said drawing my attention back to the lady she was working on, 'Madam Perdido had said she thought you would make a fantastic healer, but that you do need to meditate more. Here - give me your hands' and she placed my hands over the head of the lady and then placed hers on top. 'She is just about to come round'.

And so she did. It felt amazing - like my Aura was being caressed and like my energy was being reborn. From that moment onwards I was hooked. I listened to every word that came out of Nimbs mouth like it was the most important thing in the world. When my hour was up with Nimb, we all went for lunch. While we were at lunch Nimb gave me some symbols to work on.

Sei Hei Ki

The mental and emotional symbol pronounced 'say-hay-key'

Helpful for healing emotional or mental stress amongst other things.

Cho Ku Rei

The power symbol pronounced 'choh-koo-ray'

Nimb said to draw this on your hands mentally, to boost healing - and also to mentally draw it over your patients while healing them to keep them safe.

Nimb said there was another symbol for distance healing and that she would show me that another day but just to concentrate on these two for now.

After lunch, I partnered up with Alice. Her manner was very caring, and I could feel that in her energy. I also helped by holding Alice's hand in a healing share. She said this can make the healing stronger - and again it felt amazing. When my time was up with Alice I hugged her and said I could see why she loved doing this so much.

Next, I got to spend some time with Flick. She was more light-hearted, very powerful but was very matter of fact about it. She spoke the whole way through about nonsense, and then suddenly said in a dramatic, jokey voice 'We have a survivor. Quick stick your hands on his head or heart'.

I did so quickly, and - pop - just like that he came snapping out of his coma. Wow it felt so different to the feeling with Nimb, but still very amazing.

****

Chapter 18

I couldn't wait for the next day, and thought that I wouldn't sleep, but the pods are so amazing. I slept like a baby. I got up along with Alice, Flick, Angeleek and Evannah. We met Nimb in the cafeteria, had some breakfast then went off to the hospital.

'You girls did amazing yesterday. You can try some healing today if you like? When we are done with our first lot, we will come over and help you bring yours around'.

We all agreed that we would love to.

When we got to the hospital, Nimb showed us how to ground ourselves - and prepare ourselves so that we didn't take on any negative energy. She said, you only want your positive energy feeding into them, not theirs coming back at you. This was the bit I found tricky as I wasn't very good at meditation, but Nimb said I would get better with practice.

'For now just make sure you surround yourself in a healing white light all the way around your body and secure it neatly so there are no seams or gaps and then you are good to go'.

My first patient was a young man. I asked his name and was told it was Nathaniel. It helped me to personalise him. I couldn't heal just a lump of meat - I wanted to know who he was. I spoke to him while I was healing him, telling him all about myself and the mission and what had happened to his planet. I could feel my hands tingling as I placed them over him. They felt sort of like pins and needles, and then after a while I could feel Nathaniel's energy beginning to shift. It started to flow with the energy that was coming from my hands. It felt really nice, like a gentle babbling brook, clean flowing water flowing happily along the stream on its way to who knows where - and then suddenly I could feel the sensation that had happened when I helped Nimb yesterday. It took me by surprise and when he started to come round I yelled for Nimb. I didn't know what I was supposed to do next.

Nimb came running over. She thought something was up, and when she got to us and saw Nathaniel coming around, she said 'Wow Maggie that's impressive'. She smiled at me. 'What was with the yelling?'

'I didn't know what I was supposed to do next'.

She laughed at me, and when Nathaniel was fully awake she started to explain to him what had happened.

'I know. Maggie has already told me' he said. Nimb looked at me in confusion.

'I was talking to him while I was healing him' I said, thinking I had done something wrong.

'My word' she gasped. 'You are a telepathic empath'.

'A what?' I said.

'A telepathic empath. It's quite self-explanatory really, but I have never met one before - only read about them! Well Maggie, this is re`ally interesting'.

We gave Nathaniel a cup of Nimbs tonic and one of her cakes and he thanked me and said it was nice getting to know me! It felt good, but strange and then Nimb took me over to her patient and we bought hers around together. Then Nimb showed me how to give the patients ailments away. We shook our hands and then placed them into the soil. I could feel Nathaniel leaving me.

'Now you are ready to start another' she said. 'Would you like a tonic first? Are you drained at all?'

'No' I said. 'In fact, I feel alive. Does that sound silly?'

'Not at all' said Nimb. 'Shows you are doing it right' and then she took me over to my next patient.

I healed Henry and then a young girl with the same name as me. Alice had healed the young girls mum Violet earlier this morning, and she was asking for her daughter.

Her energy was so bubbly and fun, and when she came around she hugged me and said 'I love that we have the same name'.

That felt really special, and then she asked for her mum, so I picked her up and carried her over to Alice to ask where she was.

Alice said 'Oh my, you are a cute little thing. Come on. Let's go and find your mummy'.

We found Violet and then got a bed for Maggie next to her, but when we checked in on them before lunch, Maggie's bed was empty and she was curled up in her mother's bed. They were both sleeping peacefully. It was so adorable.

Alice said, 'you think that they would have had enough sleep' and we both laughed.

'I can really see why you love doing this Alice' I said.

Alice smiled. 'It's the best feeling isn't it? And you are very good at it Maggie, but then you are really good at anything you put your mind to'.

We linked arms and met up with the others. Before our food came out, Nimb brought us all over some tonic.

'Where do you find the time to heal and make this?' I asked.

Nimb said 'I find it relaxes me when I get in. it helps me to unwind'.

After we had eaten, we went back to the ward and I healed another three people before the day was up. Nimb suggested that we should all do some yoga and meditation when we got back - that it would be good for all of us to get into a habit of doing this. It was actually really good fun and after the yoga I found Nimbs guided meditation easy to follow. She said that you can practice at night by listening to your breath. And concentrate on the in and out.

'Nothing else. Just the in and out of your breath, and If you feel your mind wandering, you just keep coming back to focusing on the in and out of your breathing' she said.

That night after dinner I told the girls I was going to go to bed early to practice what Nimb had said.

Next morning I woke up and the others were laughing at me.

'What?' I said.

'Nothing' they all said, but I knew something was coming. I knew they had been up to no good.

We went and did some more healing every day until the last person had come around. While we had been doing this, Addy and Brad had been liaising with the government on plans to keep their planet safe. They had been using social media a lot. Obviously, they couldn't be seen, otherwise Soquil would have had a shock. Seeing Brad and Addy from different planets - that would have taken some explaining, so Jane had been in front of the camera.

They had also done a training package for teaching purposes, aimed at 6 – 9yr olds, 9 - 12yr olds and 12 - 16yr olds. They had been very busy. Dan and Mikka had gone up to make sure the repair was intact and informed us that you would never have known there had been an issue. The day before we were due to come home, Jane had said she wanted to show us something while this side of the planet was still evacuated.

She said 'Put on your hiking boots. I have had the chef make us a pack up for lunch'.

We went out into what would have been the forest and it was spectacular. The leaves had started to grow back on the trees and flowers were poking up here and there. This side of the planet was still sparse, but it was coming back to life. We even heard a bird singing and you could hear grasshoppers rubbing their back legs. We sat under an old oak tree and had our lunch and just as we were packing up, we saw a rabbit. Jane quickly took a picture of it. It felt so amazing that we had been a part of saving this planet.

Later that day, we met Angeleek and Gabe's nan. She used to go to the school, and so knew Nimb. We had dinner with her and she told us she was going to be one of the first to move back into her house. She was heading the team that was ensuring this side of the planet was going to stay safe and continue to repair. She would then liaise with Dan and let us know how it was all going and send pictures, so we could see how beautiful her planet really was. She was also going to keep in touch with Gabe and Angeleek and was to be part of the mission squad on Soquil and so was a part of the team.

Gabe and Angeleek were really pleased about this, and the next day when it came to us saying our goodbyes, it made it easier for them.

The next day, we had our breakfast and then got into our craft and into our pods. Jane, and Angeleeks and Gabe's nan shut the pods down and we instantly fell asleep. It took 3 months to get back to Waya. We had been gone for a month, but when we returned on Waya we were 7 months older and it was now July.

'Great. Just in time for exams' Gabe said.

'Cool' said both Addy and Brad. We looked at them and laughed.

When we got up to the school we were welcomed and congratulated by Professor Detronomy and Lord Raybottom, and then given our exam timetables.

'What a welcome home' I grumbled.

And so, our school life began again as if we hadn't even left. The one good thing about getting back when we did however, meant that we were in time for the Mind Combat game against the Aurals on Saturday the 20th July.

Exam time table:

EXAM TIMETABLE JULY 2019					Maggie Tucket
MONDAY	08/07/2019	9:40AM	AURA YR1	13:30PM	AURA YR2
TUESDAY	09/07/2019	9:30AM	AROMA YR1	14:00PM	AROMA YR2
WEDNESDAY	10/07/2019	9:30AM	AURAL YR2	14:00PM	AURAL YR2
THURSDAY	11/07/2019	9:30AM	MEDIUMSHIP YR1	14:00PM	MEDIUMSHIP YR2
FRIDAY	12/07/2019	9:45AM	SCENTIENT YR1	13:30PM	SCENTIENT YR2
MONDAY	15/07/2019	9:40AM	AURA YR3		
WEDNESDAY	17/07/2019	9:00AM	MIND COMBAT YR1	13:00PM	MIND COMBAT YR2
THURSDAY	18/07/2019	10:00AM	FLAVA YR1	13:00PM	MIND COMBAT YR3

****

Chapter 19

While we were out on Soquil, we had all had birthdays, but because of the timelines it meant that we were all six months older - which meant that in February I had my fourteenth birthday but by the time we got back my body and mind were now fifteen. It was all very confusing. Dan had said don't even try and get your head around it, it will blow your minds. Nimb had decided that because we had all missed our birthdays and to soften the blow of being six months older, she would throw us an un-birthday. She said it is law that when you come back from a mission you celebrate the time lost.

And so, it was set the first Saturday after we got back. Nimb and Mikka had organised with Professor Detronomy that we could all spend the night at theirs. But in the mean time we needed to revise for our exams. Professor Trixie had been very good while we were on Soquil, and even Addy and Brad had informed us of the things that were likely to be in the exam related to the mission - so none of us were at all fazed. We all had a massive advantage having put the theory behind our subject into practice. All except the Flava's exam. Addy had said she would help me out with it, and even though I knew I should be more bothered that it was my weak subject, I personally couldn't see why I would need it. As far as I was concerned it could stay my weak subject, but Addy insisted. I think this was because she had seen that next year we would be in different classes.

We were all going to be two years above our peers in Aura, but myself and Angeleek were going to also be two years above in mind combat also. Addy was going to be two years above in Flava, so we were not going to be having mind combat or Flava together next year and I think that bothered her. At least myself and Angeleek would be together in mind combat whereas she thought she would have no-one. I reminded her that she would have Brad, Gabe and Evannah.

'I know' she said. 'But it's not you guys is it?'.

I hugged her and said she could help me out and that I would try my best - but reminded her of Professor Cook's quote 'Your sense of taste is very bland'. It didn't seem very promising. But still I said I would try.

We studied hard that next week, and I have to say Addy did explain things better than Professor Cook and I could feel myself getting better. I still knew I wouldn't move up with Addy, but I was confident that I would, A. pass the exam - and B, not struggle so much next year. All the other subjects were going to be a piece of cake.

By the time Saturday approached we were all revised out, and anything we didn't know was going to remain unknown to us and so we decided that we would enjoy our un-birthdays, and our secret welcome home party.

When we arrived at Nimbs the sight was to behold. They had a giant gazebo and a tent up in the garden. They also had smaller tents around a campfire that we would be sleeping in. There were fairy lights hanging from trees and solar lights forming paths in the garden. By night-time these were going to look spectacular. There were comfy outdoor chairs for chilling and Mikka and Dan had set up a rounders section. Inside the tent the food was something else. Nimb had really outdone herself.

'It wasn't just me. I had help from these two' she said stroking Flick and Alice's hair.

'Well thankyou to all three of you' I said, 'and to you guys for the tents and garden décor. It all looks truly spectacular' I said to Mikka, Dan, Brad and Joe.

The whole gang was here, and my heart swelled with pride. We ate and drunk, chatted and played rounders. The losing team demanded a rematch.

'But this time, Maggie and Dan are not going to be on the same team' said Flick.

'Ok' we laughed. 'You put us into teams and we will play again in a bit'.

When we got up to play again, Flick put us into our teams and she had put myself and Dan on her team.

'Hey, hold up' said Gabe who was now not with us. 'I thought you said that these two were not going to be on the same team'.

Mikka laughed and said 'I think my daughter is becoming way too competitive. I will swap with Dan.

'Nothing wrong with competitive' said Dan as he moved over to what was about to be the losing team.

As night fell, the garden came to life with all the lights. We headed to the sleeping tents and sat on the logs around the campfire. Nimb had made some healthy marshmallows and some hot chocolate. She said that they had always had a tradition that while sat around the campfire they always said what they were thankful for.

Nimb said 'I think that tonight we should write our thoughts from the last year and what we were thankful for on a piece of paper. Then I will seal them in a box, and next year we should do the same thing, but also read out what we had said the year before. If anything has changed, it will remind us of how we always got to where we were'.

I thought that was such a nice thing to do. I was so overwhelmed while writing mine that I started to cry. Addy put her arms around me and did the same.

'I hope they are happy tears girls' said Nimb coming over and hugging us both.

They were very happy tears. After we finished our hot chocolates and the fire had started to die down, we all went to bed. It had been a lovely day/evening, and I went to bed fully content. I was really looking forward to chapel tomorrow. I had so much to tell my grandfather.

We all slept like babies and the next day at chapel I chatted non-stop to my grandfather. I didn't come up for air.

Every now and then he would say 'and breath'.

When it was time to go, I wasn't ready to leave.

'You do know you can come and visit me in the Hall of Minds don't you?'

'No, I didn't know that. Nobody had said'

'Well, I think they like to separate you from emotional ties in the first year, so you don't miss your family so much. They then slowly leek your feelings back in. By then you are used to being apart so it doesn't matter. But seeing as you are doing missions and the like, and you are going to be in higher classes next term - I don't think they will mind me telling you this'.

'I will go there Wednesday after my exam and let you know how they are going' I said

'That's a date' said my grandfather. This made me smile as he used to say this when I was younger and I was going to stay over with him. This memory came flooding back and filled me with warmth.

I stuck to my word and visited my grandfather in the Hall of Minds, and while I was there, I remembered the encounter I had with Addy before the mission. I was so tempted to take a peek at my past-lives, but decided I had way too much going on at the moment. My exams were going well. I had found them all so far non-eventful. I knew I had passed them, and I suspected I had passed them well.

I told my grandfather all about them, and we chatted some more about the mission. He always seemed really interested in everything I had to say. That was another memory of him right there. One of the things I loved about him when I was younger - he would listen and make me feel like I was the most important person in his world. I loved that man so much.

I went back to the dorm, and Addy was waiting for me.

'Where have you been?' she said.

'I've been visiting my grandfather in the Hall of Minds, why?'

'Because they have just announced that they are going to have an end of exam party, and I was looking for you and couldn't find you' she said.

'Ahh did you miss me?' I teased.

'Actually, yes I did. This is the first time I have not been able to find you when I wanted to tell you something'. She really was stressing about not being with any of us next year in Flava's.

'Addy, you will be fine. You will have Gabe, Brad and Evannah' I said. 'Look, let's go and find Nimb and see if she can give us a meditation class before we go to bed and see if Alice can make you a tonic'.

Addy agreed, so we went and found Alice who was with Angeleek. We told them we were going for some meditation and they decided to join us.

When we got to Nimbs, she had already gone for the night.

Alice said 'don't worry lets go find professor Willow. She will love to give us a class'.

And so we did, and by the end of it we were all feeling very relaxed. We went back to the dorm and Alice made Addy a tonic. She had calmed herself right down and we went off to bed. We finished the first week of our exams with very little drama.

The weekend flew by, and before we knew it we were back to exams. Addy had had me revising Flava all over the weekend. Myself and Angeleek had managed to sneak off to do a bit of practice for the upcoming mind combat match with the rest of the team and Dan. But apart from that it was Flava, Flava, Flava.

Angeleek had said at the mind combat practice 'you really are a good friend to Addy you know. I can tell you are not interested in Flava one bit'.

And she was right, I wasn't - but Addy meant the world to me and I wanted to make sure she was happy and if that meant sitting through monotonous boring Flava revision with her then so be it. It was only going to be for the weekend as the exam was on the Thursday and then there would be no more we could do.

And before I knew it, I was in the Flava exam, and everything Addy had taught me paid off. It was a doddle. I went and found her after lunch and thanked her.

'Oh goody' she said. 'Why don't you see if you can get in on the year two Flava exam?'.

'I can't Addy. I have year three mind combat'.

'Oh' she said.

'And anyway, even if I did, there is no way I will be able to do year three so I wouldn't be with you in that class next term anyway Addy.'

'I know' she said. 'But if you had done the exam and thought you had passed, I was going to flunk the year three paper'.

'Oh Addy' I said rubbing her head. 'What are we going to do with you?'.

The mind combat exam was a doddle and a fab way to end the exams.

That night the dining hall was set up all fancy, and after we had eaten, the tables and chairs were pushed back, and we had a DJ and music. We danced our socks off into the night.

'I wonder when they will release the results?' said Addy.

'ADDY' we all sighed

'What?' she said.

'Can't you just enjoy tonight?'

She laughed and we laughed with her.

When the music stopped, we carried on dancing to imaginary music all the way up to our dorm. Friday was a free day, and Saturday was the mind combat match against the Aurals. This was going to be a little harder than our first match against the Flava's, but we were the better team. We still didn't want any surprises, so we went for a training session in the afternoon. When we got there the Aurals were already in the hall, so we went back at 5pm.

The session went well, and we were more than ready for tomorrow, but we still decided to get an early night.

As it was the last match of the year, Lord Raybottom had decided to come and watch. The Aural's went first and got there team back in 47 minutes and 17seconds.

'They seemed really strong' said Oswald

'We better up our game in the second half if we want to beat them. No pressure, but the Aura's never lose'.

'Oh great. That fills me with confidence' said Angeleek.

'We got this girl. We just saved your planet for crying out loud' I said, and we both high fived.

When we got out there, it was harder than I imagined. The Aurals really were showing us what they were made of. I really thought at the end of the match that they had beat us and when the results came through on the tannoy, a loud roar went up from the crowd and our team.

'Only just' said Oswald. 'We really need to practice more next term. That was almost embarrassing'.

'Yes, but it wasn't though was it said Gabe. 'And you won't be here next year anyway, wlll you?'

Oswald skulked off.

'That told him' I said

'Yer I know, but he has a point. One second!! That was close'.

Monday was the end of term and we had a four-week break. Nimb and Mikka had said we could go and stay with them. They had left the tents up and there were plenty of beds in the house if it rained or was cold. We all agreed and thanked them.

'You are so good to us strays' I said to Nimb.

She just laughed and said 'you are all on the mission team. Like it or not, you are family now'.

I hugged her and said see you Monday.

****

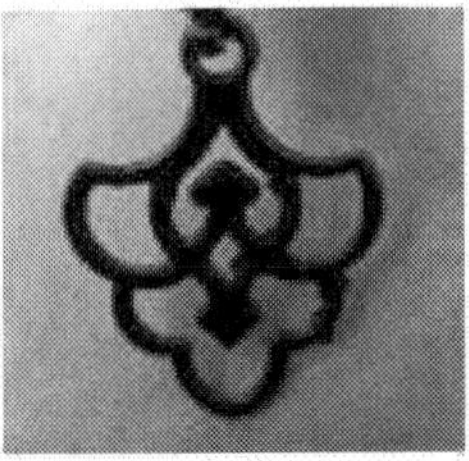

Chapter 20

Sunday night, Alice informed us that Professor Detronomy was going to let us go back to our dorms on Sundays to get a change of clothes for the next week.

She had said, 'we can't let poor Nimb wash all your clothes'.

We all packed excitedly. A whole four weeks off with the best people in the world. No school, no exams and no saving planets.

Two weeks into the holidays, we all got an envelope containing our exam results. We had all passed everything. I got 'A*' for everything except Flava's, which I got an 'A' in.

'This is thanks to you' I said, waving my Flava result in front of Addy and giving her a big hug.

Addy had got over her fear of not having any of us around in the Flava class next year. Her and Evannah were becoming good friends as well as sisters. It occurred to me that while we were on the mission, she didn't really spend a lot of time with the others. She was with Brad a lot, but he was a boy - and when we were all together, she always had me, Alice or Angeleek with her. So now she was getting to spend more time with her sister as a friend. It was lovely to see. They had a special bond forming between them.

Nimb said that we were all so dedicated and deserving and that she would host another party. I started to think that Nimb liked throwing parties.

Nimb and Mikka decided to put all the lights and marquee back up and have the party in the garden. The weather was still so good, and it was nice to spend the day and night out in the fresh air.

We all helped in one way or another. I was helping Nimb with the food as I thought that it would help next term with my Flava class.

'Wow, there is enough food here to feed an army' I said to Nimb.

'Well, if we are hosting a party we might as well have the whole team over had we not?' she said with a wink.

The evening was such fun as always and later we all cuddled up around the campfire, just chatting and chilling. Joe jumped up as someone was driving up the drive.

'Who is that?' he said.

Mikka went out to see who it was. It was Lord Raybottom. Mikka brought him over to the camp fire.

'You are all going to have to hear what Lord Raybottom has to say' he said looking a little concerned.

Lord Raybottom announced that a report had just come in that there is a problem on Yana.

'Van Allen's belt that orbits Earth has swollen and is leaking dangerous levels of radiation, effecting planets that are orbiting it. As only Yana is inhabited, that planet is our priority' he said. 'You can enjoy the rest of the summer but then we must set up a mission before the radiation reaches Yana'.

'Great' said Gabe. 'So much for a quiet life next year'

'No rest for the wicked' said Flick. This made us all laugh. As serious as this was, after the last mission we realised that a sense of humour is everything.

As the holidays came to an end, and we were packing up our things to go back to school, Nimb hugged us all, and said 'remember to build happy memories along the way'.

THE END...

Printed in Poland
by Amazon Fulfillment
Poland Sp. z o.o., Wrocław

56281100R00106